"Follow me!"

Leaving the shop on the run, the heavy bag full of pirated cassettes staggering him, Gadgets obeyed Blancanales's shouted command and fell into step behind him.

A street thug left the midday shadow of a stall, and Gadgets watched as the one-eyed man closed in on Blancanales. A bayonet from an AKM flashed in the man's hand.

Swinging his gunnysack, Blancanales knocked the enemy blade aside. Then Gadgets saw Blancanales raise a claw hammer and bring it to a bone-cracking stop, claws first, in the thug's skull. Blancanales did not break stride as he whirled, jerking the steel claws of the hammer free from the blood-fountaining skull, and continued forward through the screams and panic-filled shouts of the thick crowd.

A shape flashed at Gadgets's side. He felt the blade.

Then another thug attacked.

Mack Bolan's

ABLE TEAM

ABLE TEAM
Tech War

Dick Stivers

A GOLD EAGLE BOOK FROM

W☉RLDWIDE

TORONTO • NEW YORK • LONDON • PARIS
AMSTERDAM • STOCKHOLM • HAMBURG
ATHENS • MILAN • TOKYO • SYDNEY

With special thanks to
Ivan Chan

First edition June 1985

ISBN 0-373-61218-4

Special thanks and acknowledgment to G. H. Frost
for his contributions to this work.

Printed in Canada

1

Sirens screamed through the evening chaos of Ratnam Road. Disanayake leaned on the horn of his air force jeep and accelerated around a transit bus letting off passengers. Headlights flashed past him, a three-wheeled auto-rickshaw swerved away, then the jeep shot through a pall of diesel smoke. He saw the flashing red lights of the ambulance go east on to Kumaran, then continue on to Mawatha Road.

No! Not his friends! Not a bomb at the air force headquarters! Disanayake floored the accelerator, whipping through the traffic, the horn blaring, headlights flashing to warn the pedestrians and the drivers.

But the ambulance continued past the high-rise offices of the Inland Revenue Service and on toward the fort.

Disanayake saw nothing extraordinary in the wide avenue in front of the air force headquarters, no ambulances, no crowds gawking, no soldiers taking positions. The lines of smoking buses and trucks, the shuttling minivans sped past the headquarters building. He had been at the scenes of several bombings. No traffic would pass a scene of death and dismemberment; it was against human nature.

The sentry recognized Disanayake and motioned for the other soldier to raise the striped steel pipe barring the entry to the grounds the headquarters occupied. Disanayake saluted, then low-geared past the offices to a parking place. Workers leaving the construction site of the new headquarters building filed past him, their coarse jackets and sarongs stained and crusted with concrete dust. Soldiers accompanied the workers to the gate, herding the laborers with motions of their FAL rifles.

"What has happened?" Disanayake asked a soldier. "I heard an ambulance pass."

"Nothing here," the soldier answered, shaking his head.

Disanayake waited until the last of the workers passed before walking to his commander's office. When he arrived, an aide announced his arrival and ushered him into the inner office. Captain Wijayasiri greeted him in English.

"Lieutenant! How did it go at the airport today? All very routine, I trust?"

"Yes, sir," Disanayake answered. "But there were very few tourists. Very few proper tourists. The hippies still come. But I have yet to see a charter group."

Wijayasiri nodded. "The terrorist bombings. Terrible, and bloody devastating for the tourist industry. If we could only somehow prevail upon the newspapers to refrain from announcing those incidents to the world. I heard of a tourist asking how we succeeded in rebuilding the airport so quickly. The foreigner mistook our airport for Madras! Can you imagine? Can you imagine! Not only do we suffer from the crimes of our Tamils, now we must bear the burdens of what occurs in India!''

"But then again, sir," Disanayake added optimistically, "many of the foreigners do not associate the terror with our country. The civil disturbances in India overshadowed many of our troubles here. We are fortunate in that."

"Yes, perhaps," the captain said as he glanced at a paper on his desk. "But now, to the matter at hand. I have another assignment for you."

Disanayake felt his heart race. He swallowed hard and came to rigid attention. Had the air force finally recognized his ambition? Would he receive his long-sought and often-petitioned-for transfer to the electronics maintenance unit? After a year of duty at the international airport, checking incoming luggage and cargo for explosives, Disanayake now chain-smoked cigarettes throughout the day and experienced unceasing nightmares throughout his nights. Would he finally be released from that dreadful duty?

How far his hopes had fallen! When he joined the air force—before the escalation of the Tamil insurrection, before the riots, before the bombings—he had hoped to continue his education in electronics and make a career in computers at the expense of the air force. His parents had assembled the twenty-five thousand rupees to "arrange" his entry as a lieutenant. His future seemed assured. Though he had signed a contract for twelve years of service, he knew that another payment of twenty-five thousand rupees would buy his freedom. He anticipated four, five or six years of training before leaving to start his own factory.

But then came the civil war. Lurid images of burning shops and charred corpses appeared on the television screens of the world. The international tourist agencies took their charter groups to other countries. His father and uncle's tourist business failed. Now the few hundred rupees Disanayake earned every month went to buy rice for his brothers, sisters and cousins.

His hopes of education and training faded. His dreams of a career were supplanted by nightmares of bomb blasts leaving him blind and limbless, a hulk of suffering insensible meat with no future beyond years of isolation and an inevitable miserable death.

And his engagement to his beloved Malini.... How could he marry her when he could only bring the shame of poverty to their marriage?

How far his hopes had fallen. As he waited for Captain Wijayasiri to speak, he wished for nothing more than a transfer to a desk, even duty as a sentry. Any position that did not require opening luggage and crates and shipping cases.

That had been how the officers in Madras died, how the others had lost their arms and legs, their vision....

"It seems there are three Americans coming to our country," Captain Wijayasiri finally told him. "It is, as those Yanks say, an 'undercover assignment' for their customs office. Some affair with computers. I thought that you would leap at this opportunity to use your training with these Americans."

"Yes, sir!"

"It is an unofficial duty. You will not be in uniform. They will pay for everything. You will act as guide and interpreter."

"Yes, sir!"

"And who knows? Perhaps this could serve to advance your interests in electronics."

"Yes, sir! When do they arrive?"

"Tonight." The captain glanced at his gold watch. He slid a paper across the desk to the lieutenant. "Would you mind returning to the airport and waiting for their flight to arrive? That paper contains a list of shops and auto-rental agencies. If in the course of their duties they need services, you will direct them to. . .to my friends. Did you not work as a tour guide? Think of yourself as a guide again. You understand the arrangement?"

"Yes, sir." The lieutenant carefully folded the list and placed it in his uniform pocket. If his superior officer wanted to receive a twenty percent commission on the goods and services the Americans required, Disanayake had no objections.

At least as a chauffeur for visiting Americans, Disanayake would not be risking death or mutilation.

"I hope you will display all the wonders of our beautiful country to our American visitors—Mr. Stone, Mr. Pol and Mr. Wizard."

Disanayake nodded. For the first time in months he felt free of fear.

2

As the United States Air Force jet slowed to a stop, Lieutenant Disanayake rode a truck-mounted passenger ramp across the expanse of empty, water-sheeted runway. The lights of the jet and the blue overrun beacons lining the runway shimmered on the black mirror of the asphalt.

The monsoon rain soaked his polyester shirt and slacks. Standing on the steps below Disanayake, two porters and a soldier chattered, oblivious to the rain and the speed of the truck. The soldier's Type 56 Chinese Kalashnikov hung from his shoulder by its sling, his right hand casually gripping the gas cylinder, the receiver and plywood stock extending behind him.

Slowing, the driver neared the jet and eased the ramp toward the fuselage. Lieutenant Disanayake rushed up the steel steps and immediately saw there would be a problem.

Because the ramp was designed for the disembarkation of passengers from full-sized commercial jetliners, the level of the platform stood higher than the small plane's door. No one could descend the ramp without a ladder or another ramp. Disanayake looked down into the cabin of the jet as the door opened.

Silhouettes blocked the interior light. Men looked up at him, then down at the asphalt.

"Gentlemen!" Lieutenant Disanayake called out. "If you will have a moment's patience, I will call for another ramp. Only one moment—"

"That's all right," a voice answered. "Forget it. We can deal with it."

One of the silhouettes dropped out of sight. Then Disanayake heard the sound of sheet metal flexing. He saw a man in a sports coat climb down the side of the truck cab. The porters and soldier broke into laughter and excited Sinhalese conversation. The driver leaned out the window to watch.

"Go to the man!" Disanayake ordered as he descended the steps. "Stop your foolishness and be of service to our foreign friends!"

They rushed to help the American. One porter slipped on the oil-slick asphalt and fell. The other porter reached up to help the American, but the American's shoe caught in the porter's belt and both men fell.

The soldier stood over the tangle, explaining to the fallen porters that some foreigners believed they never needed help.

In the glow from the jet's wing lights, Disanayake saw holster straps crossing the shirt of the American. The American wore a concealed pistol. Standing, he straightened his wet coat and extended his hand to the lieutenant.

"I'm Wizard," Gadgets Schwarz introduced himself. "You're our liaison?"

"Yes, Mr. Wizard! I am Lieutenant Disanayake."

"Disanaka? Is that how I say your name?"

"Di-sa-na-ya-ka. My superiors assigned me to be of assistance to you. Please, if you will advise your associates to wait only a few moments, this distressing matter will be resolved. It is hardly necessary to scamper down like—"

"Heads up!" came a voice from above.

A shape loomed overheard, and the American Disanayake was talking to reached up and steadied a shipping trunk hanging from the jet's door.

"Down slow!" Gadgets said.

The porters reached up to grasp the trunk. One of the men took the handle, and the voice above shouted, "Hey! Don't pull on it! Quit it!"

Gadgets grabbed for the handle, but the trunk crashed down on the porters. They cried out as they fell to the asphalt, and one man grunted with the full weight of the trunk.

"Oh, wow, man," Gadgets exclaimed. "This is not safe. Lieutenant, get these dudes organized, will you?"

"Dudes? What is a—"

"Them!" the Wizard shouted, pointing at the two men struggling to their feet on the tarmac.

In rapid Sinhalese, Disanayake ordered the porters to allow the foreigners to handle their own luggage.

The porters protested that foreigners did not come to Sri Lanka to work as porters.

The soldier added that the mishap had, in fact, been the responsibility of the foreigner in the plane who released the strap suspending the trunk.

One porter complained of an injury and said he would speak to his supervisor.

The truck driver protested the foreigners climbing on the truck, which might damage a very expensive vehicle entrusted to his responsibility and perhaps cause a demerit on his employment record.

A second man dropped from the jet and shouted, "Back!"

The porters, soldier and driver went quiet. This angry American did not look like a tourist. Lieutenant Disanayake stepped forward, his hand extended for a polite greeting in the manner of men of the British Commonwealth, but the blond American rudely shouldered him aside.

The American picked up the heavy trunk with one hand. The porters commented on this in Sinhalese. How strong! A weight lifter. It seemed like nothing to him.

"Don't fucking touch it, locals! It's dangerous!"

"Lighten up, Ironman. This is Mr. Stone, Lieutenant Disanayake," the Wizard said.

"Don't give me any shit, these jokers will vaporize us," Carl "Mr. Stone" Lyons replied.

"Hey, you're lagged out and raging. They don't know what's—" Gadgets looked at the Sri Lankans standing around him. Then he spoke in a language Disanayake did not recognize. *"Ellos no saven que es adentro."*

"Yeah, yeah. Okay." The wide-shouldered Mr. Stone motioned the soldier and porters back.

The Sri Lankans watched as a third foreigner lowered other shipping cases to the two Americans standing below. The porters continued complaining of the loss of work and the driver protested whenever a case touched his truck.

The soldier suggested that the porters prepare a complaint for review by the Ministry of Labor.

One of the porters approached the lieutenant and demanded to be paid despite the problem.

Lieutenant Disanayake assured them of their pay.

The porter then demanded indemnification for the insult to their competency.

The lieutenant offered to double their pay.

The porter demanded the pay immediately.

The lieutenant took fifty rupees from his wallet and paid the porter.

The second porter immediately demanded his pay and indemnification.

The lieutenant pointed to the fifty-rupee note and told him that money would be for both of them.

The first porter laughed and pocketed the money. He ignored the other porter when he asked for his share.

The second porter argued with the first porter and the lieutenant as the truck driver simultaneously demanded a hundred rupees for damage to his truck.

"But you don't even own the truck," Disanayake protested.

The driver threatened to report the lieutenant to
the Ministry of Tourism.

The soldier joined one argument, then the other,
pointing from the jet to the truck to the Americans
to the trunks.

Carl Lyons turned to the soldier. "Set the safety on that AK," he said firmly. The soldier did
not understand. The American turned to the lieutenant. "Tell that man to set the safety on his
rifle."

In Sinhalese, Lieutenant Disanayake requested
the soldier to inspect his rifle and determine if the
safety lever had somehow fallen to the "fire" position, and if the lever had fallen, to please resecure
the lever so as to relieve the concern of their foreign
guest.

Without looking at his Kalashnikov, the soldier
objected to a foreigner commenting on a military
matter. After all, the soldier had made no threatening gestures. He continued speaking, commenting
on the strange attitudes of tourists who come to a
country and assumed they had the right to question
military matters of security forces who maintained
the peace through their diligence and courage. The
many casualties in the war proved that the military—

"What's the argument?" Lyons asked. "Tell
him to set his safety, or I will."

"Slack off, Ironman. *¿No quieremos problemas, sí?*"

"That joker is pointing an AK at me! Set your safety!"

The soldier commented that the giant foreigner seemed to make even more noise than his awkward and unsightly form seemed capable of producing. Then his voice suddenly stopped.

Grabbing the soldier by the shirt and lifting him from his feet with one hand, Lyons jerked away the Kalashnikov with the other hand. He dropped the soldier and pushed up the rifle's safety lever. He did not return the Kalashnikov. He hung the rifle on the ramp, out of the reach of the soldier.

"Radical," Gadgets muttered. "Before things go dinky dau, I think I'm gonna give you some Valium."

Lieutenant Disanayake gave the soldier fifty rupees, then turned to the Americans. "Please, gentlemen, no more disagreements. Let's hurry through the customs office and the inspection of your luggage so your visit to beautiful Sri Lanka may—"

"Customs inspection?" Lyons asked, incredulous. "You think we're tourists?"

At that moment, Lieutenant Disanayake experienced his first doubt as to the relative safety of his new assignment.

But then again, he reassured himself, these strange Americans, despite their rudeness and violence, could not be as dangerous as high explosives.

3

A horn bellowed repeatedly and headlights came up from behind them and flashed past.

Carl Lyons reacted first, jerking sideways in the minivan's front seat, his right hand reaching for the Colt Python concealed under his coat.

But the driver of the speeding vehicle did not slow, and the car's horn faded into the darkness of the Asian night.

"Do not be concerned," Lieutenant Disanayake told his American passengers in his lilting British accent. "Though others may risk their good health through reckless disregard of the highway conditions, I will continue to motor at a safe and reasonable speed. Before I joined the armed forces of my country, I worked in the tourist agency of my family. I know the concerns of foreign visitors. Safety first, is what I say. Safety always."

"He must've been doing a hundred klicks," Gadgets noted. The Able Team electronics specialist watched the rain and darkness float past. Brick and concrete shops lined the highway in what seemed to be endless rows. Bare incandescent bulbs blazed inside a few of the one-story rooms, revealing scenes of people talking, working or listening to cassette players. Where a few feeble streetlights lit a town, the light brought the palm and tin sheet roofs of small houses out of the darkness.

"What was that word, Mr. Wizard? A hundred klicks?"

"One hundred kilometers per hour. On this road. In the rain. With cows wandering around. Very extreme!"

Lyons interrupted the talk. "Lieutenant, when did you get this assignment?"

"Only this very night, Mr. Stone. A very hurry-up affair, I think."

"Yeah," Lyons agreed, his voice slow with fatigue. He looked at his watch. "It's 1:00 P.M., California time. Twenty hours ago, I was in L.A."

"And one-thirty in the morning, Sri Lanka time. What is the word, 'elay'?" Disanayake swerved to avoid a bus parked in a flooded section of road.

"Los Angeles."

"Oh, now I understand. Initials of the city's name. I will have much to learn, speaking with you gentlemen. You speak a somewhat different English than I."

"We're Americans. We speak American. What do you know about our job here?"

"Oh, very little. Almost nothing, in fact. I know only that you fine fellows represent the customs ministry of the United States of America and that you are in the midst of an investigation of some matter to do with computers. What matter that is, I do not know. Perhaps you can inform me so that I can be of service to you in your duties."

"What is your specialization in the air force?" Lyons continued his questioning.

"I have no specialization, Mr. Stone. Due to the disturbances in my country, I have forgone my training and advancement. I now have security duties."

"Security?"

"At the international airport, examining the personal belongings of tourists and articles shipped by air."

"Searching luggage? For what?"

"For explosives. The examinations employ a very sophisticated electronic device that can detect any trace of an explosive."

"Oh, man," Gadgets said in the back seat. "Not the work I want."

"Nor I, Mr. Wizard. But it is my duty. A man must do his duty."

Lyons looked at his partners. "So you got this assignment because you were a tourist guide?"

"Also because of my English-language education and my experience in electronics. My superior officers thought I was uniquely qualified to be of assistance to you."

"Did they issue you a pistol?"

"No! That would be entirely inappropriate, do you not agree? In the United States, I know the authorities routinely carry revolvers for self-defense, but here it is entirely unnecessary, except for officers posted in areas of known danger."

"Tenemos un perdedor," Lyons told the others.

"What language is that, may I ask?"

Rosario "Mr. Pol" Blancanales answered. "My friend thinks he speaks Spanish. Lieutenant, did your officer explain that there might be some danger involved in your assignment as our liaison?"

"Danger? Why? I cannot understand why there would be danger."

"Four men have died already. Murdered."

"A pity! How very unfortunate. Who were the poor souls?"

"Two truck drivers in San Francisco," Lyons answered. "An informer in a smuggling gang. And an undercover customs agent. All murdered by the gang."

Lieutenant Disanayake laughed. "I assure you, my friends, Sri Lanka is not San Francisco. There is no danger here."

Parked trucks and jeeps appeared in the headlights. Soldiers in raincoats, carrying FN FAL rifles and Kalashnikovs, waved the minivan to a halt. Lieutenant Disanayake rolled down the window and called out to one soldier. The soldiers crowded around to the window. Speaking in Sinhalese, the lieutenant motioned to the three foreigners in the van.

Able Team heard the words, "Stone... Wizard... Pol."

"He's introducing us!" Lyons said with a shake of his head. *"Un perdedor!"*

The soldiers grinned and nodded to the Americans. Then the lieutenant put the van in gear and accelerated away from the roadblock. Blancanales spoke again.

"Lieutenant Disanayake, our presence here was to be a secret. Didn't your officers tell you that?"

"A secret? Unfortunately, now the secret is out. I do wish you had informed me of your concerns."

Gadgets laughed. *"¡No creolo! Este perdedor es un comedia!"*

"Stop it!" Blancanales told his partners. "Lieutenant, as of this moment, we are businessmen touring Sri Lanka. If anyone asks about our business, tell them we are looking for a site to build an electronics factory."

"But is that not in fact why you three gentlemen came to my country?"

The men of Able Team looked at one another, and then Lyons answered the question.

"No."

4

A tower of glass and reinforced concrete, the Ceylon Intercontinental offered views of the city's metropolitan center and the Indian Ocean, the expanse of sea extending unbroken to the horizon and beyond. If the eyesight of a guest could follow the curve of the earth, the Ceylon Intercontinental would advertise views of Antarctica. But guests saw only the vast expanse of monsoon-whipped whitecaps and historical Colombo, known to the people of Sri Lanka as the fort, or Colombo Fort, because the city stood on the foundations of the fortifications built by the various colonial powers. Several imperial powers, European and Asian, had maintained garrisons on the strategic hill overlooking the natural harbor. First came the Sinhalese invaders, followed by the Tamil kings of India, then the Arabic traders, then the forces of Portugal, the Netherlands, and finally the English.

Now government buildings and tourist hotels took the place of the ancient battlements. The Intercontinental Hotel, and the surrounding development of shops, delicatessens and restaurants, occupied what had been the southwest section of the English walls.

Before the disturbances of 1983, foreigners crowded the luxury complex of hotel and shops. Limousines and Mercedes buses shuttled between the Intercontinental and the international airport. The tourists, usually from Western Europe and Australia, but on occasion from the Communist Bloc and the United States, did not need to step from the air-conditioned complex. Glass-enclosed walkways led from the hotel to all the shops. Guests had the option of breakfasting in their rooms or taking an elevator to the lobby and walking to a nearby French pastry shop or a British-style delicatessen. The glass walkways and the tables of the eateries viewed the tropical flowers of the hotel landscaping.

However, the disturbances ended that. The tourists no longer visited Sri Lanka. For several months, the management maintained a pretense of normalcy.

Then one evening a young man parked a taxi at the entrance and ran to another waiting taxi.

The blast from the bomb-rigged cab shattered the windows overlooking the gardens. Government leaders denounced the terrorism in the Sri Lankan media and refused visas to international correspondents who applied to cover the story. The management replaced the glass with sheets of imported Plexiglas.

But the tourists did not come. The hotel remained as colorful as its advertisements, but as motionless.

This night the Englishman in the rented car had

no difficulty spotting the few foreigners on the grounds. Four men sat in a van parked on the circular drive. Four others lounged in the entrance to the hotel, as if watching for an arriving group. And others stood at the corners of the block, their black plastic raincoats glistening with rain.

The Englishman smiled in the ironic manner of his people, the smile actually the grimace of a mask. His hands revealed his anxiety. On the steering wheel, his long delicate fingers moved like white worms. From time to time one hand caressed the other as he visually checked every position of the waiting foreigners.

As though he were washing, the Englishman stroked and caressed one hand over the other. Then he gripped the wheel with his right, jerked the car into gear with his left and accelerated away.

He wanted to be far away when the Americans arrived.

5

"Tomorrow I will take you to the free trade zone. That will provide you with an opportunity to establish your identities, as they say in the James Bond novels."

"Understand us, Lieutenant!" Lyons told him. "We're not three James Bonds. We don't drive sportscars and we don't romance women on government time. Our work is often violent. Sometimes we've had to defend ourselves and sometimes people have died. Did your air force give you basic weapons and combat training?"

"Oh, yes. Certainly. It is required that we learn to shoot."

"Great. And another point. When our office requested the establishment of a liaison team for this operation, they emphasized that this would be secret. Who assigned you to us? Who is your superior, what is his rank and where does he stand in the security forces of your country?"

"Captain Wijayasiri directs the daytime posting of air force men at the airport. He is a very good fellow, and all the other officers certainly respect and honor him."

Blancanales asked the next question. "Does he report directly to National Security Minister Lalith Athulathmudali?"

"I congratulate you! An excellent pronunciation of a very difficult Sinhalese name. But alas, humble Captain Wijayasiri does not hold a rank that enjoys the privilege of working with the distinguished Mr. Lalith. He is only a captain with many responsibilities."

"Lieutenant," Blancanales continued, "would I be correct in assuming that our request for a liaison officer—and the explanation of our mission to your country—passed down through a line of officers?"

"Yes, certainly. I believe the term is 'chain of command.' But Captain Wijayasiri is entirely trustworthy, a selfless servant to the country who harbors not an ambition contrary to his sworn duties. Let his selection of myself be an example of attention to his responsibilities. If you are to present yourselves as enterprising businessmen searching Sri Lanka for the site of your electronics concern, how better to present yourselves than accompanied by a certified tourist guide? I am certified, you can be sure."

"Certified!" Lyons said with a laugh.

"No doubt about it!" Gadgets added.

An army truck appeared. Switching on the interior light to reveal the three foreigners, the lieutenant slowed for another checkpoint. But this time the soldiers did not approach the van, preferring to remain in the shelter of a plastic tarp stretched over poles. They saw the foreigners and waved the van past.

"If Sri Lanka's so cool," Gadgets asked, "why all the soldier boys?"

"The Tamil Tigers. They are terrorists. We must protect the people."

"Why didn't they check us?" Lyons looked out to see a gray, wind-chopped expanse of river. "We could be a special hit team hired by the terrorists to blow this bridge."

"But my dear friend!" The lieutenant laughed at the question. "How could you be a Tamil terrorist? You are not a Tamil, it is plain to see! So therefore, the soldiers did not inconvenience you with an interrogation."

"Exactly. That's why the Palestinians hired Japanese to murder Israelis. Why the Iranians got blacks to murder Americans. Why the Soviets got a Turkish fascist to shoot the Pope. The art of war is the art of deception, a Chinese warrior-philosopher wrote three thousand years ago."

"But we are not at war with the Chinese," the lieutenant responded, obviously confused. "Nor with the Palestinians, the Iranians or the Soviets. We have no fear of terror from those nations."

The highway entered the gray, monsoon-swept sprawl of Colombo. Streetlights appeared, illuminating the stark walls of three- and four-storied buildings. Electric signs, in English and an alphabet of swirling interwoven symbols, advertised restaurants, shops and dealers of Japanese electronics. Filth and trash filled the gutters and spread across the broken sidewalks to stand in drifts against the walls.

"Is that Sinhalese writing?" Blancanales asked, pointing to a sign.

"Yes, very much different than your own, is it not?"

"And Tamil? Any of these signs have the Tamil alphabet? Our guidebooks said the languages had entirely different alphabets."

The lieutenant hesitated to answer. "You will not see any Tamil signs. They are gone."

"Gone? Why are they gone?"

The question made the lieutenant laugh. "Gone to ashes. After the disturbances, all the shops with Tamil signs were no more. The vengeance of the Sinhalese knew no limits."

"Yeah," Lyons commented. "We read about the riots of 1983. Some terrorists up north killed twenty soldiers so the people down here burned a few hundred families. Burned them alive and looted their things. And your soldiers and police wouldn't help the innocent people. Do you wonder why you've got terrorism now?"

"That is all past now. We have a new national policy of reconciliation. But the terrorists will not accept peace. They only want to kill."

"Maybe the vengeance of the Tamil Tigers knows no limits," Lyons responded, paraphrasing the lieutenant. "So this is beautiful downtown Colombo. Where are we staying?"

"The resplendent Hotel Intercontinental, the standard of gracious and carefree accommodation, featuring the conveniences of knickknack shops and barbers and auto-leases—all within steps of your luxurious rooms. How fortunate you are to visit in the off-season. If you were to have come in August, at the time of the Kandy Perahera, you would not be so fortunate. Rooms are reserved months in advance! Many visitors are very sadly disappointed.''

The concrete-and-chipped-stucco buildings became a metropolis of neo-1950s architecture intermixed with crumbling buildings in the style of English slums. In the city center, soldiers stood in front of the closed banks. Police slept in cars parked at taxi stops. The lieutenant whipped the van through a maze of one-way streets, finally slowing as he came to a boulevard lined by high-rise offices.

"Stop!" Lyons told him. "Stop here."

"Certainly, but why?" the lieutenant said as he jerked the van to the curb. "The hotel is there, only another block."

Lyons turned to his partners. "Witnesses of the truck killings remembered Orientals in the area of warehouse?"

"Couldn't give descriptions," Gadgets added. "But remembered nonspecific unidentified Orientals. Why?"

"Like that one standing in the rain?" Lyons indicated a form in a black plastic raincoat. "Looks Korean or Manchurian. As we turned the corner, I saw him talking to something in his hand."

Lieutenant Disanayake threw the van into gear

and accelerated. "Do not fear, my friends! I have my security officer's identification. I have full authority under the law to question anyone—"

And he braked to a stop in front of the Korean.

"Don't!" Lyons whispered.

But the young Sri Lankan threw open his door and stepped out. The Korean did not register surprise as he saw the Americans. He called out as his right hand brought up a square object concealed under his raincoat. His left hand swept open the snaps to expose the muzzle of a mini-Uzi.

Startled at the sight of the rising weapon, Lieutenant Disanayake fell back.

Then Lyons fired an X-headed .357 Magnum hollowpoint into the Korean's face.

6

As Lyons took the steering wheel, Blancanales threw open the side door and stepped out. Lieutenant Disanayake watched the dead Korean collapse on the sidewalk, his brains a vast splash of gore on the rain-slicked wall behind him. Blancanales grabbed the Sri Lankan officer and threw him back into the van.

Tires shrieked and the grisly scene receded as Lyons accelerated backward. In the headlight beams they saw forms in black raincoats. Lyons hit a switch to cut the headlights as the van gained speed.

A muzzle flashed a hundred yards away. Lyons attempted a backward right turn and lost control of the van. The buildings and streetlights revolved in a slow-motion panorama of plate glass, neon and gray concrete until a wheel slammed into a curb. Blancanales broke a side window with his head, but he held on to the lieutenant. Then the van spun in the opposite direction as Lyons clashed the gears.

"Don't wreck it!" Gadgets screamed. "Get us gone! I don't want no Commie Koreans chasing me nowhere!"

"You ever worked a stick shift with your left hand?"

Gadgets threw a canister out of a window. Lyons managed to find the proper gear position and the tires shrieked again. Purple smoke spread behind them as the van careered around a corner.

"Excellent evasive driving," Blancanales commented as he shoved the sliding door closed. "Lieutenant, are you all right? Can you hear me?"

"My head...." Lieutenant Disanayake rubbed his ear with the palm of his hand. "There is a ringing."

"No shit, man." Gadgets commented. "Nothing like a Magnum banging to get it ringing. Then again, that DK gook had an Uzi that goes like one two-zero-zero-nine milos to the minute and You—" Gadgets jabbed a finger into the center of the lieutenant's chest "—were first in line."

Lieutenant Disanayake only looked at the jiving American, not even attempting to understand him. "What a terrible surprise that was. Who would have thought that fellow would be concealing a machine gun?"

Lyons laughed. "Could have been worse!"

"How could it possibly be so? That unfortunate fellow certainly died."

"Could've been you."

"Ah, yes... very true. One must consider one's own well-being. That man was a Communist? Did you recognize him from an intelligence dossier?"

"Forget him! Give me some directions! We've

got to get off the street before the cops put out an APB.''

"Yes, the police. We must go to the police. Make a turn at that road—''

Now Gadgets laughed. "We didn't come here to talk to cops. Where's another hotel? Someplace we can hide out, no questions asked.''

Taking the list of shops and businesses from his jacket pocket, the lieutenant shook his head. "There was no provision for another hotel.''

"Hey!" Lyons shouted back, startling the young officer. "Get with it! Deal with the situation. Someone set us up. They know about us, and they know about you. You saw that Korean bring up the Uzi? He had shoot-on-sight orders. Shoot to kill. They find us, it's more trouble. Trouble that you might not live through if you don't get very good at dealing with it very fast. We need a house or a hotel or an apartment. Somewhere with an open area nearby, the size of a parking lot, a baseball field, whatever, no wires, no trees. Think!''

"Oh, you are a sports enthusiast!''

Lyons groaned. Gadgets laughed.

"Yes, I know a place. It is very close. Near the air force headquarters. And there is a soccer field where helicopters arrive—''

"Helicopters?''

"Do not fear! Helicopters come very infrequently. They shall not disturb your rest. There is perhaps more noise from the motorcars. You will find the hotel very quaint, yet comfortable.''

CARL LYONS WOKE to a wailing voice. Staring into the darkness, he realized he was listening to a loudspeaker amplifying the morning prayers from a nearby mosque. He had heard Arabic prayers in Egypt, Lebanon and Syria. He checked his watch. Four in the afternoon Los Angeles time. Four thirty-five in the morning, Sri Lankan time.

Did he have to get out of bed? He had slept only three hours. The freighter would not arrive for another two days. Or three. Or four. As they had flown from the United States, he and his partners had agreed to sleep through the first day to adjust themselves to the complete reversal—from day to night—of their bodies' biological cycles.

But they had not anticipated the shooting at the Intercontinental Hotel.

The Colombo police would be searching for the gunman who had killed the Korean. In his jet-lagged mind, Lyons reconsidered his assumption that the Asian with the Uzi had been North Korean. The man had looked Korean. Lyons knew Koreans from his years on the Los Angeles police force. Able Team's mission briefing had noted the presence of operatives from the Democratic People's Republic of Korea. However, the briefing memos did not define the role the North Koreans played in the theft of the argon ion laser and the mainframe computer that directed the ultraprecise tool. Perhaps he would never know.

The mission directive did not mention an investigation; it referred only to the laser and mainframe.

INTERCEPT OR DESTROY.

If Able Team failed, the President would be forced to order the destruction of the components by air or naval attack, even if the destruction of the components meant sinking a Soviet or ComBloc freighter.

The call to prayers finally ended. Four forty-five in the morning. In the darkness, he heard rats skittering in the room's cabinets. Lyons turned in the bed, the straw mattress under him crackling and releasing a smell of dust and human sweat. He touched the modified-for-silence Colt Government Model on the bed beside him. Could he risk another few hours of sleep?

Had the police gotten the license number of the van? No, he'd raced away too fast. Had anyone seen the three Americans in the van? Probably not. The Korean had stood alone in the rain. How could the Colombo police search for the unknown gunman without a license number or descriptions or a motive?

If the police somehow linked the three Americans to the shooting, Able Team would be in jail today.

Considering the angles and leads, Lyons, with ten years' experience as a detective, gave the local police no chance of making arrests.

Unless that lieutenant screwed up. But Blancanales had Lieutenant Disanayake in his suite. The naive officer would not get the opportunity to inadvertently or deliberately inform on Lyons and his partners.

However, the Koreans would be a different threat. They had expected Able Team at the Intercontinental Hotel. The Koreans were probably searching Colombo for the American unit now, but they would be looking for the Americans in the high-class hotels. Not in a decayed hulk of a hotel smelling of filth and rotting carpets.

Lyons decided to sleep. At least until daylight.

BLANCANALES OPENED HIS EYES with his hand already closing around the grip of the Beretta 93-R selective-fire pistol. In the semidarkness of the hotel suite, he saw the white-shirted form of Lieutenant Disanayake sit up on the next bed.

The noises of traffic continued outside; motorcycles whined, buses clattered and rattled, trucks sounded horns. Blancanales listened. What had woken him? A sound in the hallway? Feet on the balcony? A tool against the window?

Then came the sirens. An eerie chord created by the sirens of many ambulances rose from the city.

"A bombing!" The lieutenant spat out a Sinhalese phrase.

"What?"

"A bombing! Somewhere in the vicinity. In the fort. Perhaps they attacked the government buildings. Or perhaps the railway station. I will—"

A knock interrupted the lieutenant. "It's the Wizard! Open sez me," a voice said softly.

Going to the door, the lieutenant pushed aside a table, slid back a bolt, then turned the key to unlock the door. Gadgets entered with radios in each hand.

"I was listening in on the police frequencies and guess what? I heard the bang and then it was crazy city. Everyone screaming for ambulances and soldiers and priests. Sounds real bad."

"Mr. Wizard, how can you have a police radio? It is prohibited by law!"

"Everything fun's illegal. What I've got is a multiband scanner operating. Monitors all the frequencies and lets me skip from radio to radio. News crews in the U.S.A. use them. 'Another woman driver got machine gunned from her seat—film at eleven!' But I understand absolutely zero of your Sing-hala lingo and the Brit lip ain't too clear, either. Only thing I understood was that it was Laksalas—whatever that is—got wasted."

"Brit lip? Lingo? Ah, I understand. How unfortunate! Yet Laksala is only a tourist shop. And at this hour—" the lieutenant glanced at his watch "—it is closed. May I listen? I will learn the details and report to you, my friends."

Gadgets explained how to operate the miniature unit. "Push this button when you want to change channels. This way up frequency, this way down. It goes to the top frequency then starts over on the lowest frequency."

"You want to let the Ironman know about the bombing?" Blancanales asked.

Going to the balcony, Gadgets threw open the French doors, then the shutters. Gray dawn light lit the room. "No way, man. He told me only if it was an emergency. And a body count on postcards and souvenirs ain't serious. You saw how he acted at the airport. Good thing he got the chance to pop that Korean. Released some of his aggression.''

Sirens screamed past the hotel. Gadgets shut the glass doors. ''Room with a view, you got here. I view a cow, a garbage dump, crows, beggars and all these dudes wandering around in long dresses. Colombo, the City of Drag.''

''Sarongs, Wizard. Asians were wearing woven sarongs before Europeans took off their animal skins.''

''Can't I tell a joke without getting a lecture? It's hot, man. Let's get this cooler going.''

Turning the air conditioner's power switch, Gadgets leaped back as the machine seemed to explode in a clattering of metal on metal. He twisted the switch off.

''*¡No bueno!* And this place'll be a sweat box in about an hour. Not my idea of a hideout.'' As he spoke, Gadgets took off the plastic grille of the air conditioner.

''It was in fact the shop of Laksala,'' Lieutenant Disanayake told the Americans.

''Was there anything on the killing last night?'' Blancanales asked.

''Call for poison gas!'' Gadgets shouted as he pointed into the air conditioner. Roaches swarmed from the unit, and he stepped on the insects, each one dying with a distinct crack. Then he grabbed one of Blancanales's shoes and beat at the roaches.

''Kill them on the floor, Wizard! I don't want to look at that mess for the next week.''

"Abstract art, man."

Blancanales ignored his partner's antics. "What about the killing, Lieutenant?"

"There is no mention of that."

"Then continue monitoring that scanner. We might have both the police and the Koreans searching for us."

The lieutenant glanced at his watch. "We should listen to Radio Sri Lanka; they broadcast in English and I believe you may find the news of my country very interesting. There may also be news of the bombing. Do you have a radio that will receive civilian transmissions?"

"Dig it, kid." Gadgets rushed out of the room. "I got everything!"

The telephone rang.

"Are you expecting a call?" the lieutenant asked.

"No!" Blancanales said. "You answer it. Answer it in your language and remember, we're not here."

Lieutenant Disanayake spoke in his fluid, musical language. He turned to Blancanales. "Would you like a breakfast of rice and curry or fried eggs American style with—"

Blancanales motioned for Disanayake to put a hand over the telephone's mouthpiece. After the lieutenant covered the phone, Blancanales said, "Please! Remember that I spoke German last night. Remember that you told them we are Germans? We do not speak English. Don't speak English when the hotel people can hear you. And nothing American style!"

The lieutenant uncovered the phone and spoke loudly in German, then spoke in Sinhalese again to the kitchen. After he hung up, he reported, "I told them my German friends would like the best breakfast the cook can make, with very generous portions and very quickly. I am sure you will have a ravenous appetite after your long flight and—"

"Please understand our situation, Lieutenant!" Blancanales said, struggling to keep his cool. "Eating is not our number-one concern."

A few minutes later Gadgets came in with an all-broadcast-band transistor radio. "Is this the channel? All I'm getting is disco music."

"What an excellent radio! You Americans are so wealthy."

"Stick with us, Louie. We've got only the best."

"That is the morning music program. I often listen to that music myself." Glancing at his watch, the lieutenant said, "Only another moment."

They listened to Asian renditions of American disco music until the program announcer signed off in Sinhalese. Then came a musical theme of violins and percussion instruments, followed by a frenzied beating of drums. An electric tone beeped and the British-accented voice of a woman announced. "It is 8:00 A.M. This is the Sri Lankan Broadcasting Corporation. Here is the news, read by J.D.L. Sothinatham."

"First, the headlines..." the lieutenant told them.

"Only minutes ago, the Eelam terrorist gangs internationalized their campaign of murder by setting a bomb at the Laksala shop in Colombo Fort. Police report several persons dead and others wounded. India accuses a plot by a, quote, foreign hand, unquote, in the drought ravaging the central provinces. Nuclear scientists of Sri Lanka receive international acclaim in the utilization of atomic energy to increase the digestion of straw by water buffaloes by treating straw with urea."

"What?" Gadgets asked, incredulous.

"Quiet!" Blancanales replied.

"The business information systems exhibition, sponsored by the USSR, opens today in the Hotel Taprobane."

Blancanales pointed at the radio and looked at Gadgets, who nodded, acknowledging that he understood.

"The police report continuing pranks by irresponsible persons despite repeated public appeals by city of Colombo Police Chief C. M. Kellapotha."

Metal banged against the door and the two men of Able Team moved instantaneously, autopistols appearing in their hands as they split up, Gadgets going to one side of the suite, Blancanales to the balcony doors. Lieutenant Disanayake could only stare at the suppressor-fitted Beretta 93-R automatics they held.

Dishes clinked. A barefooted waiter in a white sarong and white shirt backed into the room, pushing the door open as he balanced two trays in his hands. Setting their pistols' safeties, Gadgets and Blancanales hid the weapons behind their backs. His head wiggling in a fluid side-to-side nod, the young man smiled at the foreigners as he put the trays on the table and set out the napkins and dishes. Blancanales whispered to the lieutenant, "Tell him to knock next time. . . ."

7

As Captain Wijayasiri parked his Fiat in its assigned space in the air force compound, he saw the Mercedes limousine. A visit by a government minister, he thought. Could there possibly be an investigation of cunning General Siriwardhana? The general had contrived a clever means of smuggling gemstones to the Sri Lanka Mission to the United Nations in New York City. Though Captain Wijayasiri had attempted many times to discover the means, and therefore follow the general in success, every attempt to solve the mystery failed.

Or, he wondered, while he walked to his office, had the State Gem Corporation somehow stumbled upon the enterprise of Colonel Perara? The smuggling of geudas—a stone that became the precious blue sapphire after a heat treatment—had earned an English estate for the brilliant Colonel Perara. He often boasted of his estate, his blond German mistress, his numbered bank account. All his friends envied him. Yes, Colonel Perara had much to be thankful for. Sadly, the colonel had lost his younger brother in the first weeks of the Tamil insurrection. The young man, an officer in the Colombo police, died as he bravely fulfilled his duties, murdered as he attempted to interrogate three sinister terrorists—a woman and her two teenage daughters—who hid behind their facade of innocence and weakness until they sprung their trap. The brave young man had suffered a grotesque fate, a rat smashed down his throat. Captain Wijayasiri forced the morbid thoughts from his mind. All men die. But not all men become as rich as Colonel Perara.

Then, entering his office, he saw that he had visitors—two Europeans and a fellow countryman. His countryman, obviously irritated that the captain had not arrived earlier to receive his unscheduled and unexpected visitors, announced himself.

"I am J.K.S. Selvakumar, under secretary of the Ministry of National Security. And my distinguished friends are Mr. Verity of ExpoTech of France—"

"It is a pleasure to meet you, Captain Wijayasiri," the Frenchman said, extending his hand.

The captain noted that the foreigner correctly pronounced his name. "And a pleasure for myself, also," he replied.

"And Mr. Patrick R. Hansen of England, of World Electronics, Limited."

"Colonel Perara mentions you often, Captain."

The Englishman's words alerted Wijayasiri to the true import of this meeting, as the foreigners had no doubt intended. To confirm the meaning, he asked, "Ah, yes! Electronics. I trust the management of World Electronics often consults with the colonel in his capacity of director of the high-technology schemes of the armed forces of Sri Lanka.''

"Often," Mr. Hansen answered. "It is on his direction that we meet with you."

"As it is I who oversees the purchases of certain technology."

"Oh, yes, Captain. We know. The colonel spoke at length of you. Be assured that the colonel has full confidence in you."

Captain Wijayasiri did not continue the line of conversation. He became silent, waiting for the others to make the proposal. How much would they offer to expedite the purchases?

"Let us proceed directly to the point," Selvakumar rudely demanded. "My office instructed you to assign a man to assist three Americans. We provided instructions and an itinerary for their brief visit. Is that not correct?"

What did this mean? Did they not want to sell electronics for installation at the airport? "Indeed, yes, it is true. I assigned—"

"Why are they not where they are to be?"

"I do not understand. I assigned a certain lieutenant to serve as their driver, interpreter and liaison. I have every confidence in the lieutenant."

"Your confidence is ill founded. The Americans did not stay in the Hotel Intercontinental this previous night."

"No? How odd. I myself issued the photocopy of the itinerary to the lieutenant. Where did the Americans stay?"

"We do not know! They are gone! That is why

we are here! I demand to know where the Americans have gone!''

''When Lieutenant Disanayake reports, I will inquire. Would you please wait with your questions until he calls me with his report?''

''No! Now! It is imperative that—''

The Englishman interrupted Selvakumar. ''Please, allow me to explain, Captain Wijayasiri. Time is of the essence. It is imperative that we reestablish contact with the Americans. You see, we are deeply involved in the affair. The whereabouts of the American unit is the foremost question in our minds. I do not believe it is necessary for me to speak at length of their mission. You already know, as do we all, who are here. But allow me to stress, we *must* reestablish contact. Can you help us with that?''

''Without a doubt! When my man calls, you shall receive a copy of the report forthwith. Did you wish to discuss the sale of electronic components for the facilities of the international airport?''

The Englishman smiled. He appeared very princely. Perhaps he counted royalty among his ancestors. ''When, Captain, will the lieutenant call?''

''Today.''

''Can you possibly contact the lieutenant and request an immediate report?''

''I have only the telephone number of the Hotel Intercontinental and you gentlemen tell me—''

''He is not there. Unfortunate. Is there any other measure you might attempt to contact him?''

"Certainly! I will immediately dispatch men who are familiar with the lieutenant to inquire at the hotels of Colombo."

"Excellent!" The Englishman turned to the under secretary and his French associate. "The captain has the matter in hand. We can return to the business exposition. You can contact us there, Captain. And if you are free this evening, perhaps you could stop by our suite at the Hotel Oberoi. We market a line of marvellous airport lounge multispatial arcade-simulators, and I'm sure you will find our products fascinating. Good day."

After shaking hands again with the foreigners, Captain Wijayasiri escorted the group from his office. The foreigners smiled again and left with a friendly wave. The under secretary ignored him.

"What a distinguished fellow, that English gentleman," Captain Wijayasiri declared to his aide. "So congenial. So knowledgeable in electronics."

For his part, Patrick Hansen also had an opinion on Captain Wijayasiri. However, he did not speak until the chauffeur closed the doors of their limousine. Then he screamed out, "That bloody useless bugger!"

8

Weaving through the late-afternoon chaos of downtown Colombo, the driver of the three-wheeled Honda rickshaw ignored an onrushing CTB bus and veered across two lanes. A Fiat sedan skidded, drifting sideways through the rubber smoke of its panic stop, to rattle and crash into a post at a side street. Lyons gripped the welded frame of the rick and waited for the next thrill. Beside him on the narrow bench seat, Lieutenant Disanayake watched the passing squalor of the decaying colonial city. He pointed to a statue of Buddha screened by trees.

"On the night of a festival, it is very beautiful here. The people bring many paper lanterns and flowers. It's a pity you did not arrive only two days ago. You would have had the pleasure of viewing the May Day parades."

The driver interrupted. "Does the distinguished mister want tour of lovely city Colombo?"

Lyons looked at Disanayake, then answered the driver with a guttural, *"Ich kann nicht Englisch sprechen."*

"Want pretty Fräuleins?" The driver persisted.

Disanayake answered the driver in Sinhalese,

and the two Sri Lankans argued back and forth. The driver took his hands off the rickshaw's handlebars and made a circle with a thumb and forefinger of one hand, then plunged his other forefinger through the circle.

Taking his eyes off the traffic, Lyons studied the driver's mahogany-dark hands. Nicotine and engine grease stained his fingers, the filth coloring his calluses in mottled splotches of yellow and black, as if his hand rotted with gangrene. The filth-stained straight finger continued plunging through the filth-stained circle. Lyons looked up at the driver's leering grin. Phosphorescent red betel juice made his mouth a macabre wound filled with yellow teeth jutting from diseased gums.

Lyons pointed forward. The driver did not turn around. Lyons slammed the driver in the back with the heel of his hand. With a sneer, the driver gave up his pimp pantomime. Lyons pointed again, this time to the sidewalk. Disanayake relayed the instruction to the driver and the three-wheeler shuddered to a stop and Lyons hopped out. Standing on the curb, hundreds of Sri Lankans passing around him, he waited as the lieutenant paid the fare.

His eyes scanned the street and sidewalks. Traffic crawled past, bumper to bumper. Buses and trucks spewed clouds of diesel smoke. Motorbikes weaved through the chaos, their engines screaming with two-cycle revolutions. Noxious drifts of pollution swirled around Lyons as he checked the cars for Koreans. Or Soviets. Or whomever the KGB had hired to find and kill the three men of Able Team.

The unending rush, and the eye-stabbing, lung-cutting pollution, defeated his search for faces. He looked only for weapons pointed at him.

When a thousand horns exploded at a freight truck blocking an intersection, Lyons studied the sidewalk crowds. Men walked past in sarongs, jeans and tropical suits. Women wore traditional saris and cheap polyester fashions. The afternoon's fading gray light reduced the brilliant colors of the saris and skirts to pale halftones.

In his peripheral vision, Lyons saw Blancanales pass in another three-wheeler. Blancanales did not even glance at his partner as he continued on to their agreed destination, the Hotel Taprobane, site of the Soviet-sponsored business and information systems exhibition.

Lyons had slept throughout the day in his air-conditioned room. In the afternoon, talking with Gadgets and Blancanales, he agreed that a casual driveby of the Taprobane might confirm Blancanales's suspicion that the Soviets had scheduled the stolen argon ion laser to return to the USSR with the crates carrying the dismantled computer exhibition. Blancanales wanted to compare the dimensions of the Russian computer systems to the specifications of the American system. Lyons had wanted to get out of the decaying hotel and find a restaurant. The risk of encountering a Korean find-and-kill unit only heightened his appetite.

Now he regretted his bravado. The filth, the pollution, the stink, the claustrophobic crowding of the fort—the built-over site of various European

imperial garrisons that had become the metropolitan center of the city—sickened him.

"Let's go! It is very near."

"Don't talk English."

"Then how will we communicate?" Disanayake
asked as he guided the American through the
crowd. Lyons looked down on all the local people.
Even Disanayake, who was tall for a Sinhalese, had
to look up to him. "You do not speak German.
And I do not speak Spanish. Perhaps you could
speak in the idiom of your friend Mr. Wizard. No
one will think of him as an English speaker."

Lyons laughed. He tapped Disanayake on the
shoulder with a hammerlike fist, and the young
lieutenant flinched from the friendly strike.

"There it is. You got it." Lyons mimicked his
partner's improvisational speech patterns as they
walked. "This man's got to jive and bop. Den no
one knows what goes. But I can't. Not really.
Wizard doesn't care if people understand him. He
talks like that just to kill the boredom. I've heard
him talking in the dark, memorizing phrases that
don't make any sense to anyone but him."

"You are speaking English, Mr. Stone."

"Ich kann nicht!"

They came to Upper Chatham Street, and Disanayake pointed to a line of yellow folding barriers
ringing one of the crumbling turn-of-the-century
facades. He said only, "Laksala."

To Lyons, all of the buildings on the street
looked bombed out, ravaged by the equatorial ex-
tremes of sun and monsoons, destroyed by Asian

neglect, condemned from the moment of their completion a lifetime ago by the decadence and self-declared grandeur of the British Empire.

A few new structures relieved the decaying British influence, but the modern buildings only confirmed the fact of destruction by decay. Built in the Soviet-modern style, another empire dedicated to the subjugation of nations by military force and bureaucratic strangulation, the offices and shops already looked desolate and gray, like multimillion-dollar welfare tenements abandoned to rats and junkies.

These thoughts of the past and present flashed through Lyons's mind even as his senses continued scanning the streets and passing crowds for the enemy. Despite the noise and incomprehensible languages, he listened as he walked a step behind and to the side of the lieutenant, the shoulders and arms and clothing of the people around him brushing against his body.

A hand grabbed him. Lyons reacted before identifying his assailant, almost before he sensed the motion behind him. Seizing the arm and spinning one hundred eighty degrees, he crashed backward through people as the attacker went airborne. Lyons stopped in a short sparring stance, his eyes flicking back and forth across the jammed sidewalk, his body's sudden inertia doubling the muscles of his legs, converting his momentum into another change in direction. He sprung forward, turning, and saw the attacker.

Sprawled on the sidewalk, surrounded by laughing Sri Lankans, a crippled boy stared up at Lyons. He gripped a worn crutch in one hand as he tried to untangle a stick-thin withered leg from under him.

"You okay, kid?" Lyons crouched to help up the teenager. Holding out his hands, he spoke a word he had learned from a guidebook included in his mission briefing kit. *"Hondai? Hondai?"*

The crutch cracked against Lyons's head. The crowd gasped at the beggar boy's revenge as the boy cursed Lyons. "You shit Yank motherfucker! I want practice some English language and you break my back."

Lyons laughed. He felt a warm trickle seeping out of his hair. His hand found sweat-thinned blood. The crippled boy's face went slack when he realized that he had assaulted and bloodied a foreigner.

"Sorry, mister. I am very sorry. I should not grab you. You freak out."

"No soy shit Yank motherfucker. No entiendo que usted habla. Toma..." Lyons gave the boy a handful of brilliantly colored Sri Lankan rupee notes. A second later, he had left the boy and the knot of onlookers behind. The lieutenant ran to catch up with Lyons, then led him around a corner.

"The Taprobane is there, the imposing building viewing the harbor."

Lyons saw a hundred-year-old hotel overlooking warehouses and freight yards. Soldiers with Kalashnikov rifles paced the sidewalk in front of the entrance. Sri Lankans in business suits waited for taxis. The street ended at the chain link fence of the harbor, where barricades and a line of police sentries insured security.

"I wonder why tourists don't come here anymore?" Lyons asked Lieutenant Disanayake with a wry note in his voice.

"Yes, that is the question! My country remains beautiful, my people very friendly, the prices reasonable—despite the inconveniences of the terrorism. Personally, I believe it is the jealousy of the Indians. They pay journalists to libel Sri Lanka."

Dodging through traffic, Lyons crossed to the opposite side of the street and continued to the door of a restaurant. Inside, he saw tables and many patrons, Sri Lankan and foreign. Waiters in sarongs took trays of food from a long cafeteria counter. Lyons saw a front corner table available, overlooking the Taprobane.

He took a corner table and watched the arriving and departing guests at the hotel entrance. Disanayake sat down opposite. Glancing to the nearby diners, he leaned forward to Lyons. "You are injured, I believe. There is blood. Perhaps you should see a doctor."

"Bruce Lee with a flashing crutch," Lyons answered in a whisper, almost laughing. Dozens of voices and the noise from the kitchen covered his words. "Forget the doctor. It's already stopped bleeding."

"We have a medical aide on duty at air force headquarters. On the way back to the hotel, I could report to my captain and you could—"

"Forget that!"

"But I must report to my superior officers."

"One of your superior officers set up the ambush last night."

"That is not possible. Entirely out of the question."

"Then who did?"

"How can I tell you? It is a complete mystery."

"You were assigned to work with us, right? To work liaison? Understand, liaison in this situation requires your presence every minute of the day and night."

"But I must report."

"Look, Lieutenant. We want you to work only for us. Not for your officer. How much do you get paid in a month?"

"In a month? Oh, with benefits and bonuses—"

"How much?"

"Two thousand rupees."

"At twenty-five rupees to the American dollar, that's eighty dollars a month. Times twelve, that's about one thousand dollars a year. Tell you what. If you will follow our style of liaison for the next few days, that is, total secrecy, even from your officers, we will pay you one year's salary, in dollars. That's one thousand United States dollars. Twenty-five thousand Sri Lankan rupees."

The lieutenant stared at Lyons. Lyons turned his attention to the hotel. He watched a group of Asian and European businessmen pile into three taxis. Then he saw Blancanales cruising by the hotel in a three-wheel cab.

"That is a great deal of money, Mr. Stone. What

must I do? I will not violate the laws of my country, or compromise the honor of my position.''

"We don't want that. We want secrecy. You will do the job your captain expects of you, but without reporting to him."

"But you violate the law. And I will be with you."

"Your Minister of National Security knows what we came to do. We are in your country by his authority. Hopefully, there will not be any more incidents like last night. And last night is exactly what we don't want to repeat. That's why we need the secrecy. Think about it."

A waiter came to their table. "Good afternoon, gentlemen. Would you like to see a menu?"

"¿Usted habla español?" Lyons asked.

The waiter looked at Lieutenant Disanayake. They spoke quickly in Sinhalese, and the waiter left. Lyons watched the hotel.

"He will bring short eats."

"How about tall eats for me?"

Disanayake laughed. "Very good, a very good joke. But there will be much for you to enjoy. Short eats means something very similar to fast food in American. But I think you may find Sri Lankan food more interesting than hamburgers and hot dogs."

A group of Europeans arrived in a tour bus, wearing the baggy suits of ComBloc countries. Fat bulged over their collars. Two other Europeans left a taxi. These men wore elegant suits and had styled hair. They looked familiar to Lyons. The names

Hansen and Verity came out of his memory, and he would have to check the photos in his mission kit later. For now, he studied their features and mannerisms.

Their leather-and-brass briefcases swinging opposite to their stride, the stylish Europeans walked quickly to the ComBloc group and greeted them. The leader of the group made introductions as they all entered the hotel.

"Mr. Stone, I agree to your request for secrecy...." Lyons heard Disanayake's voice pushing into his concentration.

Lyons nodded, not taking his gaze from the hotel.

"However, I believe Captain Wijayasiri may request a payment also."

"Great, we'll pay off whoever puts out their hand. As long as we get the job done."

For the last hour of the day, Lyons watched the Taprobane. He saw Soviets, ComBloc officials, Europeans and thousands of Sri Lankans.

But no Koreans.

9

Joy filled the being of Lieutenant Disanayake. The entirely unexpected offer from the American secret agent promised to change his life, to free him from his obligations to the air force.

Never again would Disanayake serve a shift at the airport. Never again he would fear a bullet from a panicked terrorist infiltrator. Never again would he search a shipping crate for concealed explosives, his hands shaking with the fear of a booby trap and dreading the instant of white light before death, or living death in the cripple wards of the national hospital.

American dollars meant freedom.

Throughout the afternoon and evening he restrained his joy, fearing that when they returned to the hotel the other Americans might withdraw Mr. Stone's offer. A thousand United States dollars! For Disanayake. And if the circumstances dictated, another thousand dollars for his superior officer. Lieutenant Disanayake would not, of course, tell Captain Wijayasiri of the first thousand dollars. He would inform his captain of the second thousand dollars and offer to share and share alike. That meant Disanayake could hope for another few hundred dollars.

Freedom and perhaps a down payment on a tourist bus. Or a ticket to the Persian Gulf, to work in the rich Arab states.

The dollars meant opportunity to improve his life.

Disanayake allowed his imagination to fly free. Could he hope that the Americans would take him to the United States? He resolved at that moment to accept any role, to face any danger in the assistance of the cruel, joking and inexplicable Americans.

He wanted freedom.

As the evening progressed, the lieutenant doubted if he would face any dangers. Mr. Stone took a very leisurely dinner in the Nectar Café, observing the comings and goings of people from the Taprobane as he enjoyed seemingly endless quantities of food. Stone began with a plate of short eats, very quickly consuming the buns of deviled beef and fish and curried vegetables. He sampled dishes of jaggery pudding and sliced papaw, which he mistakenly thought at first to be mango. A tumbler of delicious woodapple juice amazed him. Upon determining that he indeed had a taste for Sri Lankan cooking, he ordered an á la carte dish of sambol. However, the fire of the curries and chilies caused the American great distress and he consumed a second tumbler of woodapple juice, a bottle of soft drink and finally a dish of buffalo curd, of which he did not stop to savor the topping of jaggery, cinnamon and nutmeg.

Shortly after he'd finished eating, the concealed radio of Mr. Stone buzzed with a code of some meaning to him alone and the two very different soldiers departed their table in the Nectar.

Taking a closed cab through the warm, rain-misted evening of Colombo, as Mr. Stone stared silently at the passing view of shops and pedestrians, Lieutenant Disanayake pondered his situation. This strange American, what did he think while he watched the city in silence? Did he think of the poor fellow he had killed the night before? Did he only think of his mission and his responsibilities? Did he reconsider the generosity of his offer to his companion, Disanayake? Could Disanayake dare to ask for yet another thousand United States dollars?

Everyone knew of the wealth of America, a country blessed with immense national resources. So strong that it took what it wanted from other weaker countries, the countries dominated by the American banking and military empire. How much could Disanayake win of those untold hundreds of billions of dollars? If Mr. Stone offered him one thousand, then quickly agreed to two thousand, why not five thousand? Ten thousand?

Why not a million dollars?

Lieutenant Disanayake trembled with the joy of this sudden opportunity. Wealth beyond his wildest dreams became possible. But the next thought brought the gloom of despair.

The Americans would not grant this lowly soldier, only a lieutenant, that vast sum.

But why not the Soviets? The Americans had come a great distance, on a military flight for three men only, to execute a mission of great importance to the United States. If the United States government considered the mission against the Soviets of that importance, how would the Soviets consider the mission?

Would the Soviets pay a million American dollars to succeed in the endeavor that the Americans came to disrupt? Lieutenant Disanayake knew the Sri Lankan air force would pay only a few thousand rupees for information on the activities and crimes of the American secret agents. And, after the killing, more rightfully called the murder, of the Korean, did not the Americans deserve to be called "terrorists" rather than "secret agents"?

Disanayake wondered if Mr. Stone would deal with him in that way. Instead of paying the promised dollars, would Mr. Stone discharge his promise with a bullet? Would Disanayake die dreaming of wealth and freedom?

Somehow he must contact the Soviets. Only the Russians could protect him from the Americans. And the one million American dollars? Had not the Soviets contributed endless millions of rupees to the development of Sri Lanka and other Third World countries? Had not the Soviets steadfastly supported the efforts of the United Nations?

At that moment, as the cab passed the Hotel Morningstar and wheeled through a wide circle turn to the hotel entrance, Disanayake saw the Korean.

The man wore a black raincoat and stood in the space between one shop and another, watching the covered entry of the Morningstar. Only by a freak chance of headlights and reflections had he seen the Korean's features. No Sri Lankan had a face like that. And no tourist would stand in the monsoon, watching a hotel.

Disanayake looked at Mr. Stone. The American stared at the line of beggars and cripples putting down sheets of plastic and cardboard, preparing to sleep on the sidewalk. Distracted, the American had not seen the Korean.

Disanayake did not tell him of the man's presence.

Sometime during the night, or perhaps the next day, Lieutenant Disanayake decided he would slip out of the hotel and talk with the Korean surveillance men. The Koreans would take him to the Soviets.

He would wait for the opportunity.

10

"Today, mercenary forces of the United States attacked a unit of Afghan and Soviet forces guarding the highway to the city of Herat. Fighting in defense of the nation's socialist revolution, the Afghan and Soviet comrades-in-arms defeated the cowardly assault, capturing a number of the fascist enemies and driving away the survivors. The prisoners reported their paymasters to be operatives of the American Central Intelligence Agency. Elsewhere in Afghanistan, visiting Soviets toured the new schools and hospitals—"

"Demonstrating the use of napalm and poison gas!" Lyons cursed, his Colt Government Model rising on line to the shortwave radio. "You turn it off, Wizard! Or I off it."

Gadgets backed up a step as he said in a slow, calming voice, "Set the safety and I'll switch it off, okay? Don't shoot my radio."

The Radio Moscow voice continued. "Children now enjoy medical benefits previously limited to—"

"To crematoriums and horror shows." Lyons leaned forward and jabbed the radio's power key with the autopistol's suppressor. Only the continuous drone of the air conditioner broke the silence in the room. Lyons flicked the fire selector up.

"I cannot tolerate hearing that. I do not want to hear it again."

"Cool, man. It's cool. I respect your opinion."

"Ease off," Blancanales told Lyons. "Shooting the radio won't stop the broadcast. It'll only make this room more like a prison. The radio helps."

To emphasize his point, the Puerto Rican ex-Green Beret pointed at the barred windows, the locked door, the shuttered French doors. The air conditioner's drone, a low whirring and rattling and an occasional scraping, became maddening, a sound as oppressive as the institutional green walls covered with decades of filth. From time to time, traffic noises punctuated the sounds of the air conditioner.

"How about some Kandy music?" Gadgets asked. He held up a cassette tape featuring Sri Lankan dancers in traditional costumes. "No agit-prop there. Couldn't understand it even if it was there."

Blancanales shook his head. "Not again. Get another tape."

"I could play it backward," Gadgets suggested. "Might sound better—"

"My friends!" The lieutenant spoke up. "You wish to hear music? I could go to the Pettah. For only thirty rupees, I can buy tapes of the Jacksons, the BeeGees, Abba. Of the same quality as that tape. Would that not be very pleasant?"

"How can they only be thirty rupees?" Gadgets asked. "That's only a dollar and twenty cents."

"I do not know, Mr. Wizard. I only know the price and the excellent quality and selection."

"Oh, yeah! They're pirated! Like in Singapore. Straight off the American albums. Better than the agit-dance Sinhalese disco."

Lyons looked up from the briefing folder. "Give me a break. I'm trying to make sense of this information."

"Then how about Radio Sri Lanka? Lieutenant, what time does that come on? I want to hear some more about that nuclear research on buffaloes."

Disanayake rushed to the radio to find the frequency. "Mr. Wizard, I believe—"

"Give me a break," Lyons repeated strongly.

Blancanales spoke quietly. "Why don't you give *us* a break? You don't like the program selection in this room, why don't you try the entertainment in your room? We don't mind eating dinner without you. Read in your room."

"You win, you all win. I'm sorry but I just can't stand being locked up in here, knowing that I'm in this prison because a gang of Europeans that we can't touch are ripping off America. To sell the loot to the Soviet Union."

"We don't know that," Blancanales countered. "ExpoTech is a legitimate company. Verity could be here for legitimate reasons. We'll watch. Be patient, Mr. Stone."

"You think you got it bad?" Gadgets laughed. "You slept all day. Then you went out and played tourist. I stayed here and waited for the alert. I mean, I have got that Sinhalese music memorized. I even got the harmonics of that torture machine memorized!'' he said, pointing to the air conditioner.

"Did you memorize the make-sheet on this English gangster Hansen?'' Lyons asked. "I nominate him for a serious traffic accident. Maybe we could push him in front of a bus.''

"I read through the folder but only got as far as Verity.''

"Too busy listening to your cassette player?''

"Don't tell me how to kill my time!''

"My friends!'' Lieutenant Disanayake spoke again. "Would you like me to go out for newspapers? For magazines? You could study the history of my beautiful country. I'm sure you would find it interesting. And I am certain it would contribute to the understanding of your assignment.''

Lyons glanced at his partners. He shook his head.

"We need you with us every moment of the day or night,'' Blancanales explained to the young officer. "In the event of an emergency, we would be lost without you. In fact, we cannot even order a cold drink without you.''

"Oh, but you can! Room service will answer your call until ten o'clock tonight. There will be no problem.''

"But, Lieutenant, we can't order in English,'' Blancanales repeated patiently.

"But you can! I am sure they speak excellent English in the kitchen."

"We are Germans, remember?"

"I am sure some of the fellows speak German."

Blancanales shook his head. He spoke softly, but his voice carried exasperation. "But we don't speak German. And if we're Germans, they will wonder why we don't speak German. None of us can even fake it all that well."

"But Mr. Pol, I do not understand this. Why—"

"*¡Un periador!*" Lyons laughed.

"*¡Esto goonado no entiendo nada!*" Gadgets raved. "*¡El haceme dien kai dau loco!*"

"Perhaps you can order in Spanish," the lieutenant suggested.

Even Blancanales laughed now. "Find someone in the kitchen who speaks Spanish and then you can go look for some Puerto Rican tapes for me. Agreed?"

"If I am to go to purchase cassette music tapes, I must go tonight. Tomorrow is Poya and it will not be possible."

"What's Poya?" Lyons asked.

"The day of the full moon. The Lord Buddha was born, became enlightened and died, all on days of the full moon. No shops are open; no one works on Poya."

"Except you," Lyons corrected. "Because you work for us. Twenty-four hours a day."

Dishes clinked in the hallway, and they heard the musical voices of the waiters. A hand rattled the doorknob.

"They still don't know how to knock!" Gadgets went to the door as his partners casually took their positions in opposite corners of the room, their weapons concealed behind them.

Two waiters carried in trays and placed them on the table, covering its surface. A third waiter stood looking at the table, tray in hand. He spoke to the other waiters, and the three of them, seeming identical in their white shirts and white sarongs, stood looking at the table, talking and gesturing. Finally, they started to leave without putting down the third tray.

"Hey!" Lyons said. He caught himself and switched to Spanish. *"¿Donde vayan con la comida?"*

Lieutenant Disanayake called back the waiters and pointed to the bed. The three men discussed the suggestion for a minute before setting the tray on the bed. Then they returned with two more. After a long discussion with the lieutenant, they placed those trays on the bed, too.

One of the waiters tried to set the table, but he could not find room for the napkins and flatware amid the clutter. He put a napkin in place, but could not find a place for the opposing fork. He tried again, putting the napkin in another place, setting down the knife, fork, and spoon, but he could not find a place for the bottle of a pink soft drink. He began again.

Lyons silently pushed the man out the door. After closing and bolting the door, he pantomimed shooting through the door with an autorifle. "Death to the waiters!"

"Could happen," Gadgets agreed as he took the silenced Beretta 93-R out of his pocket. "They walk in without knocking, it might be a very, very bad scene. For them. Might be a laugh for us."

11

A bellman weaved through the businessmen and government dignitaries crowding the conference hall of the Hotel Oberoi. Western representatives wearing conservative gray suits talked with Asians in conservative white sarongs. Europeans and some Asians drank cocktails. Muslims drank fruit juices. The stark colors of the men's clothing contrasted with the brilliant red carpeting and the multicolored, intricate batik tapestries draping the walls. Only the pastel saris of the few Asian women present matched the colors of the decor.

Patrick R. Hansen, the co-host of the reception, introduced three businessmen of three different continents and cultures to one another. "Mr. Singh, Mr. Ekra, this is Mr. Tikhonov of the Soviet Electronics Export Ministry. My corporation works with Mr. Tikhonov to manufacture and distribute Soviet innovations throughout the world. As you saw today, our machines equal in quality any machine offered by any other country or company. And we offer our excellent machines at prices far lower than our competition."

"Indeed," Mr. Ekra, the African, commented.

"Your machines seem to be exact copies of what is offered by IBM."

"No!" the Soviet protested. "Not true! They copied the achievements of Soviet electronic engineers. It is proved."

"Please do not judge our products by their appearance," Hansen interjected. "There are very few ways to style a rectangle and yet remain utilitarian. Consider the electronics inside the consoles. Totally different. Come back to the exhibition tomorrow. We will run more complex programs." Hansen turned to the bellman waiting beside him. "Yes? What is it?"

"You have a call, Mr. Hansen."

"Excuse me, gentlemen. I will return immediately."

Smiling and nodding his way past prospective clients, the Englishman broke out of the crowd. He rushed to a telephone with a blinking light.

"Hello! J. R. Hansen here."

A voice spoke in Russian. "Can we talk?"

Hansen saw no one near him, and he switched to whispered Russian. "Yes. Speak."

"This is Chon. We found them. They have rooms at the Hotel Morningstar on Ratnam Road. We are ready to enter."

"Wait until very late. Watch and wait. I will make calls so there will be no interference."

Hansen hung up and returned to his clients.

12

Able Team attacked their dinner, discovering new foods as they uncovered each dish. Lieutenant Disanayake told them the name of each course and instructed them on the correct style of eating.

"Red pepper!" Lyons gasped over a mouthful of food. He grabbed a bowl containing a block of ice and drank the few drops of cold water that had collected in the bottom. Then, in desperation, he mouthed the block of ice. He held the bowl to his chin, his mouth on the ice, as he seemed to french kiss the translucent block.

"It's cool," Gadgets complained, "that you want to make out with the ice. But you know, that's our ice, too. And I don't like other people's slobber in my pop."

Lyons finally set down the ice. "That is the hottest hot sauce I've ever had. Like white phosphorus in my mouth."

"I am sorry, Mr. Stone," Disanayake said with a smile on his face. "I will instruct the cooks to be more considerate in the future. Is there something wrong with your chop suey, Mr. Wizard?"

Now Gadgets was reaching for the ice, pushing as much of the block as he could into his gaping mouth, trying desperately to quench the fire that raged within. Disanayake studied Gadgets's bowl of vegetables and noodles.

"How inconsiderate! They made the chop suey with hot red peppers. I will surely protest."

"I didn't eat anything red!" Gadgets gasped. "It was green, I thought it was a vegetable. But..." He put his mouth back to the ice.

"Yes, it was a hot green pepper! All the vegetables are peppers. They must have confused our order with the order of a Sinhalese party."

Blancanales took a long strip of green pepper from the bowl. "That is the biggest jalapeno chili I've ever seen. A monster chili. You *norteamericanos* just can't eat *comida picante*."

"You eat it," Lyons dared.

A moment later, Blancanales jerked a Swiss Army knife out of his pocket and popped off a bottle cap. He gulped down tamarind-flavored soda.

"Is it hot?" Lyons asked. " *¿Muy picante?* Try some of this flat bread. It helps kill the fire."

"What is this jive?" Gadgets wondered aloud. "They gave us a block of ice and soda pop. No glasses. How are we supposed to get this block of ice into a bottle?"

Throughout the dinner, they chipped at the ice block with a K-Bar knife, putting slivers of ice into their mouths whenever the chilies and curries seared their palates. Finally, in the wreckage of dishes and empty bottles, only plates of *nan* bread and bowls of rice and vegetables remained.

"Too much. What a meal!" Gadgets said as he

fell back on a bed. "This place may seem like a prison, but you don't eat like this in a prison."

"Shame to waste all this food," Lyons commented. "What do you say I give it to the beggars out on the street?"

"I can't eat any more." Blancanales pushed away a plate of bread and rice. "Take it away."

Lyons put the flat slabs of bread on plates, then cleaned the other plates of rice and vegetables. The flat bread would double as plates.

"Just like El Salvador," the blond ex-cop commented to the lieutenant. "They serve food on bread there, *tortillas*. Eat the food, eat the plate. No waste."

Lieutenant Disanayake studied the American. "You fought the Communists in El Salvador?"

"What are you thinking? That we're a death squad? Wrong, kid. We fought death squads. Wiped them out."

"You fought for the Communists?"

"Wrong again. The death squads are murderers. Gangs of torturers. Rapists. Child murderers. Most of them get paid by the Salvadoran Nazis. But a few work for the Communists. And the people of El Salvador are trapped between the gangs. I don't talk politics to gang murderers and rapists. I put them down. Come on, let's go feed someone."

The young lieutenant looked at the three flat breads and the mounds of vegetables. "That will not be enough for all of the beggars."

"Kid, you got to do what you can, or you end

up doing nothing. Understand me? You change the
world by working a day at a time.''

They carried the bread through the dark hallway and down the stairs. The waiters and bellmen
smiled and swiveled their heads in the peculiar
side-to-side nods. One waiter saw the food Lyons
and Blancanales carried and brought a trash can.
A rat leaped out and streaked away into the hotel
restaurant. Lyons shook his head, and the waiter
followed Lyons with the trash can, not compre-
hending why the foreigner would go to the street
to throw away garbage.

Lyons stood on the sidewalk and surveyed the
beggars. The Hotel Morningstar, built during the
British colonial period, had the balconies overhanging the alley. The overhang created a shelter
from the monsoon rains for arriving and departing
guests—and for a long line of cripples, beggars and
the desperately poor.

Who would get a meal?

The legless man sleeping under his hand-driven
tricycle? The elderly man and woman sleeping on
cardboard? Lyons saw that the old woman's
ragged sari had fallen open to reveal vast pellagra
sores spreading over her emaciated back and but-
tocks and legs. The old man with the empty eye
sockets? Lyons looked at a drunk sleeping in his
vomit and walked past. Continuing down the line,
he saw misery and disease and disaster repeated
again and again, each time in a different form on a
different person. What three of the suffering people deserved to eat tonight?

One man and woman slept on the concrete, their two children, the oldest about four, the other perhaps a year younger, between them. They had folded newspapers under their children, then wrapped their children in rags and newspapers as protection against the chill of the night and rain.

Lyons stood over the family. Because of the flat bread in each hand, he nudged the sleeping man's callused, filth-crusted foot with his shoe. The man took his arm from around his sleeping child and looked up to see the blond man dressed in the expensive slacks and sports coat of a European foreigner. Lyons crouched and offered the bread and vegetables.

Boys walking behind Lyons laughed. But the unfortunate father and mother thanked Lyons with the Buddhist gesture of hands pressed together, prayer style, and a nod. They took the two breads as the street boys in sarongs laughed. The boys pointed at Lyons as he walked away. Lyons looked back to see the man and woman waking their children to the gifts.

Lieutenant Disanayake waited in the hotel entrance, the third bread in his hands. Lyons took the bread and vegetables and went to the legless man who slept beside his tricycle cart.

As Lyons woke the cripple, Disanayake watched the darkness across the street. The headlights of passing cars and buses swept past the shopfronts. Finally, a truck's taillights lit the narrow space between two shops.

The red glow revealed a form dressed in the slick

black of a plastic raincoat, watching the hotel. Disanayake waited. He would wait for the American to reenter the hotel before signaling.

As the American's weight creaked on the old stairs, the lieutenant flicked his cigarette lighter. He held the flame near his face to illuminate his features.

"What're you waiting for?" Lyons shouted.

Startled, Disanayake grabbed for the pack of Marlboros in his shirt pocket. He turned and saw the blond American standing on the stairs. "A cigarette, my friend. Mr. Pol asked me not to smoke in the suite."

Lyons came down the stairs. He stepped close to Disanayake and told him, "Smoke in the hallway. We've already spent too much time out here. It's not safe for any of us."

"Oh, yes. I understand. Certainly."

When the American turned his back, Disanayake snapped a salute to the Korean surveillance man, then turned and followed the American.

13

Lyons's bowels were on fire.

He sat naked on the toilet, spasms knotting his guts, red chilies, curries and exotic spices exploding outward. To brace himself against the pain, Lyons arched backward and gripped the pipe behind him that ran vertically from the toilet to the porcelain flush tank mounted near the ceiling. The pipe creaked with the stress as another spasm gripped his guts. The pain made sweat flow down his body.

Finally, the spasms stopped but the searing pain continued. He reached over to the bathtub and turned on the faucets. Rust-colored water came from the "cold" tap. Cold water, clouded with gray matter and bits of debris, came from the "hot" tap. He waited as rusty water spread across the bottom of the bathtub. Years of abuse and cleaning with sand had left the white enamel of the tub black-splotched and rusting.

His bowels finally empty, Lyons jerked the toilet's hanging chain. The chain broke for the third time, but the toilet flushed. Then Lyons lowered himself into the tub, the cold water soothing him. He turned off the water and lay back, staring up at the abstract smear of yellow light his flashlight beamed onto the green ceiling.

The lightbulb in his bed lamp had burned out. After five requests by the lieutenant for a replacement, Lyons had taken the bathroom's lightbulb for the bed lamp.

Above Lyons, mosquitoes orbited the flashlight glow. A finger-long cockroach scuttled into the light, then veered back into darkness. In the silence, Lyons heard strange clicking and rasping sounds coming from under the bathtub. Rats? Cockroaches? Cobras? Lyons took the flashlight, leaned over and peered under the bathtub.

Red eyes flashed and a shape disappeared down a drain in the concrete floor. The darkness of the drain moved, light reflecting from the curved backs of cockroaches retreating from the light. Lyons switched off his flashlight and sat in the darkness.

"I hate this. I hate it here. I hate this place. I hate these people," he cursed in a hoarse whisper.

Only the three tritium dots of his modified-for-silence auto-Colt broke the darkness of the bathroom. The gun lay on the corner of the tub, the phosphate blacking of the weapon's metal making the pistol invisible except for the glowing nightsights. Lyons turned and looked out the barred window. Above the black outline of a tree, the monsoon clouds glowed a faint gray with the reflected light of the city.

Lyons sat in the silence of the city's predawn. Only a few motorcycles and trucks moved now, the faint engine sounds mixing with the buzzing of the mosquitoes around Lyons.

Darkness. Silence. Peace. Flame pain. Suffering. Poya day. No one would work. A day of celebration of the Lord Buddha's birth, enlightenment and passing into Nirvana. For Lyons, Nirvana would be a novocaine enema.

A motorcycle's two-cycle whine came from the distance. To distract himself from the fire in his guts, Lyons concentrated on the approaching noise, counting the seconds to make a speed estimate. The motorcycle dopplered past the hotel in a scream of Japanese-engineered revolutions.

Sixty-something miles an hour. Maybe more. On wet asphalt. Broken asphalt. Slimy with oil and mud and filth. Cows wandering around. Unmarked roadwork and ditches. That kid is looking for his next turn on the wheel of rebirth, Lyons thought.

A rat skittered in the hallway, and Lyons opened his eyes. His bathroom had two doors. One opened from his room and the other from the hall. The bathroom had at one time been used as one of several common baths along the hallway. Double-bolted and blocked by a washstand, the hallway door had not been used in years.

Under the hall door, through the built-up filth and hair, Lyons saw a faint light. The light swept from side to side. He heard no footsteps. He waited for Gadgets or Blancanales to knock and identify himself. They had eaten the same food. They must be awake, too, sweating and groaning on toilets or pacing as the pain seared their bowels. Maybe Blancanales had some painkiller to share.

No knock came. Lyons closed his right hand around the grip of the auto-Colt. He thumbed back the hammer and set the safety. With the first hollowpoint round in the chamber, he had eight shots.

Lyons eased out of the bathtub without a sound. Finding the flashlight with his left hand, he dripped across the concrete floor to the bathroom's inner door, which opened onto his room. He pressed his naked back against the slick plaster of the wall and waited.

Weight crashed against the door. But the cross bolt and lock held. At the opposite end of the hallway, other doors banged. An instant later, another banging cracked again and again, like high-velocity hammers slamming the heavy wood door. The doorknob bounced across the room. Lyons saw light through holes in the door, then ducked back as slugs ricocheted from the floor and punched the furniture.

The door flew open. Two dark forms rushed in, both with flashlights held against the forestocks of sound-suppressed submachine guns. A continuous rain of brass casings fell on the floor as the assassins swept the room with autofire, the unending slamming of slugs into concrete, bedding and chairs covering any noise escaping the silencers. The flashlight beams moved from side to side in smooth arcs.

Putting his flashlight down in the doorway, Lyons grabbed a can of shaving cream and threw it into his room as he fell to his left. On his side on the floor, he clasped the auto-Colt in both hands and lined up the tritium dots on the back of a silhouette's head.

His auto-Colt bucked once, the silhouette jerking, a mist spraying from the head as the other form turned. Slugs cut across the bathroom's doorway at waist height, hammering the plaster and brick walls, splintering across the door. Clicking down the auto-Colt's fire selector, Lyons triggered a 3-shot burst and the assassin's flashlight popped. In the sudden darkness, he heard breath exploding from a chest, the next breath a choked gagging sound.

As broken glass tinkled, Lyons moved. A motionless cone of light came from one of the assassins' flashlights. Lyons saw one form sprawled across his bed. Nerve spasms jerked the dead man. Lyons saw brains and a staring, dangling eye where a face had been. The other man gasped on the floor, struggling with his left hand to reach a pistol shoulder-holstered under his left arm. Pink bones gleamed from the ruin of his right arm, blood jetting in pulses. Lyons reached down and took the Korean's pistol.

A boot toe slammed into Lyons's thigh and he fired his Colt even as he fell. The maimed, semiconscious Korean had high kicked, bringing down the man who had wounded him. But the burst of .45-caliber hollowpoints reduced the Korean's head to fragments. Lyons sprawled across the corpse of the other Korean, feeling hot gore smear his body.

The Colt had chambered the last cartridge and Lyons moved fast. Not stopping for clothes, he grabbed the web belt hanging on the corner of the bed. He dropped out the empty 7-round standard magazine from his Colt and jammed a 10-round extended magazine up the well. He looped the web belt over his shoulder as he rushed to the door. Crouching there, listening for other Koreans, he buckled the web belt around his naked waist.

Crashing came from other rooms, and Lyons withdrew a stun-shock grenade from the belt. Designed for commando assaults against terrorists occupying schools or airliners, the grenade exploded in a blinding, deafening flash of white light. But the cardboard casing produced no deadly fragments. The grenade produced temporary insensibility in every terrorist and hostage within the confined space of a room or aircraft. Lyons straightened the safety pin with his thumb as he listened for movement.

A rectangle of light appeared as a room door opened. Stepping into the hallway, a square shouldered, tanned man called out in a German-accented voice. "Stop that goddamned hammering! Stop it immediately! Stop or I will stop you!"

The German knotted the belt of his dressing gown as he shouted. In the German's room, Lyons saw a naked Sinhalese boy leave the bed. The boy stepped into a sarong and tied it around his waist.

Three slams came from the far end of the hallway.

"Do you hear me?" the German shouted again.

"I want that hammering to stop or you will be stopped!"

Slugs ripped through the air, slapping into the German's chest, spinning him. He fell gasping, choking on blood in his throat. The Sinhalese boy screamed. Lyons heard the boy throw open the room's French doors. The balcony railing creaked as the boy climbed down to the street.

Lyons waited. He saw a shadow shift. The black form of a Korean stood near the stairs. Still holding the stun-shock grenade, Lyons braced his left arm against the doorframe to support his auto-Colt as he aimed. He squeezed off one shot.

The Korean lurched, falling back against the wall, then staggering forward, slugs from the suppressed submachine gun in his hands chipping the plaster walls, splintering doors, ricocheting the length of the hallway. Decades of dust clouded the hall as the last slugs went into the ancient carpet.

Lyons waited, the Colt on line. The hand radio hooked to his web belt clicked twice, then twice again. Lyons answered with two clicks, then one. Finally Gadgets keyed his code, two clicks, then three. Lyons set the stun-shock grenade down at his feet and unhooked the radio.

"This is the Ironman," he whispered. "I'm okay."

"Wizard here. More scars on this walking scoreboard, but the visiting team lost."

"I got them as they came through the door," Blancanales told his partners.

"I just put down another one by the stairs. You see any others?"

"Saw that one hit the dust," Gadgets answered. "But I can't scope the hall without sticking my head out."

"Pol, the lieutenant still in your room?"

"He's one very nervous young soldier," Blancanales told the others. "I don't think he's ever been in action. And who was the man in the robe?"

"Forget him," Lyons muttered. "He mouthed off for the last time. We've got to get out of here. Watch the hallway while I put on some clothes. Put the lieutenant to work packing."

Two minutes later, leaving his packed and locked shipping trunk in his doorway, Lyons eased into the hallway. He had buckled on his web belt under his sports coat. Leaving his auto-Colt holstered, he now carried one of the Koreans' Heckler & Koch MP-5 SD-3 submachine guns.

Lyons stepped over the dead German and switched off the room light. By the gray light from the avenue, he crossed the room to the balcony doors and slipped outside. On a balcony to his left, two men whispered to each other in hurried voices.

Crouching behind a planting box of flowers, Lyons scanned the avenue. He could not see the entrance of the hotel, but he could see parked cars on both sides of the avenue. Directly in front of the hotel, a truck idled, the cargo doors open. Black forms stood at the truck, submachine guns in their hands.

Lyons keyed his hand radio and whispered, "We

got more of them out front. With a truck. Waiting. What do you say I get them moving, quiet, so we can get out of here?''

"That's all we want," Blancanales answered. "This isn't a body count mission."

"Waste them!" Gadgets told Lyons. "Can't chase us. Can't come knockin' if they're dead."

"Got no argument with that," Lyons said as he pocketed his radio.

Lyons sighted on the nearest Korean and triggered a long burst, wasting ammunition as he swept the line of slugs across the truck and into the body of a second man. He shifted his aim to the driver's door and fired, knowing he could not hit the man, but scoring on the door and the rearview mirror, glass shattering, metal banging, deformed slugs humming away into the distance.

A black form sprayed the balconies with silenced autofire, slugs clanging off the iron railings, ripping past Lyons to break roof tiles. Lyons fired a long burst into the Korean's chest and face, emptying the H&K submachine gun's magazine into the falling gunman. As he changed magazines, he heard the truck accelerate away as the unfortunates on the sidewalk under the balconies shouted out in panic. Lyons keyed his hand radio.

"Watch the hall. I'll be coming toward you."

Moving quickly through the shadows and dim light, Lyons checked doorways. He stopped at each of the several common bathrooms and pulled the doors closed. For some reason known only to the Sinhalese management of the hotel, the bathroom doors had bolts on the outside. Lyons secured each bolt. If a Korean had hidden in a bathroom, he did not want him suddenly appearing from behind.

At the stairs, the dead Korean lay in a vast blood-stain. Lyons snapped a glance down the stairs, saw no one. He hooked a chair with his foot and sent it smashing and bumping down one flight. No one reacted. Lyons dashed across the open space.

Gadgets signaled his partner with a quick, "All right!" Leaving his doorway, Gadgets ran to the dead man and jerked the body back into cover. He stripped off the Korean's bandolier of 9mm magazines. "Righteous! More ammo."

"You ready to go?" Lyons saw blood on his partner's shirt and slacks. "Where are you hit?"

"Everywhere! Don't even ask where I was when they came busting in. Or how I lived through it. It's too embarrassing."

Lyons laughed softly. "Don't need to ask. I know all about it."

14

In the last hour of night, the sky black with monsoon clouds, Able Team crossed the Victoria Bridge over the Kelani River in a stolen tourist van. Disanayake drove close to the sentries guarding the bridge and shouted out, *"Airportekata!"* In observance of Poya, the soldiers did not leave their circle around a cassette player. They waved the van past without a document check.

They continued north through the darkness and stillness, leaving the urban sprawl of Colombo behind. Unlike their drive on the highway two nights before, they saw no Sri Lankan pedestrians. No one would work the shops and factories this morning. Only wandering cows and dogs used the road.

After carrying his shipping trunk of gear to the stairs, Lyons had slipped out of the hotel with Disanayake to drag the dead Koreans into the lobby. Lyons had cautioned the lieutenant against opening the garage where he had parked the minivan. Lyons explained, and the lieutenant immediately understood why they must find another vehicle. The Koreans had not come to take prisoners. Entering the garage or starting the van risked triggering a bomb. A three-block walk to a travel agency's parking lot had produced another van. Despite the dead German, despite the black-clothed corpses stacked behind the reception desk, no police came to the hotel. Able Team loaded their equipment and sped away into the Asian night.

The lieutenant said nothing as he drove north. At an intersection marked with signs in the swirling brush strokes of Sinhalese, he turned west. The high beams illuminated overhanging trees and the vertical columns of coconut palms. Cows looked out from ditches on the sides of the narrow road. In the glare of the headlights, a distant bull seemed luminescent.

"That cow's glowing in the dark!" Gadgets pointed. "Think it could be one of those atomic experimental cows?"

Passing through a town named Wattala, they saw lights inside houses. The sultry predawn air smelled of frying peppers and fish.

"Red pepper..." Lyons groaned.

Gadgets shone a penlight on a tourist map of Colombo. The map ended at Wattala. He flipped the sheet over and searched through the provinces and national highways until he found Colombo, then the Kelani River.

"This doesn't have the detail, but as long as we don't go north, we'll be within range of the transmitter. Disanayake, is this tourist resort close?"

"Yes, very close. We will come to the guest houses momentarily."

"And there's no chance," Lyons stressed, "that there'll be other people there?"

"As I said before, Mr. Stone, I do not believe so. My family did not have the funds to complete the scheme. The caretaker may remain on the premises, but perhaps not today, because today is Poya, day of reverence for our Lord Buddha. If the caretaker is not at the development and no one else happens along, we will be alone."

"Until the caretaker comes back," Lyons countered.

"Then I will simply tell him I persuaded three gentlemen tourists to visit. Though the conveniences are not complete, the location is very scenic and naturally pleasant. You will see and undoubtedly agree."

"And perhaps," Blancanales added, "after this you will have the money to complete your guest houses."

"Yes, yes. I will certainly hope that is so."

Rain struck like a wave, beating the van's roof, flowing over the windows. They felt the van sideslip on the suddenly flooded asphalt, but the lieutenant reduced speed without losing control. He continued in a lower gear.

"We have umbrellas?" Blancanales asked.

"Can't carry everything," Lyons answered.

Gadgets looked out at downpour through the headlights. The rain seemed to create a wall of water. "Takes me back to when—"

"Forget the Vietnam nostalgia," Lyons interrupted.

"Hey, it's all I've got. You can talk about playing college football. I played search and destroy in monsoons like this."

Suddenly, Gadgets shouted, "Stop! Let me out!" Tearing off his sports coat, he threw the sliding door aside and stepped into the rain. His partners saw him splash through a flooded ditch and disappear into the bushes.

"¿Tourista?" Blancanales asked Lyons.

Lyons laughed. "Napalm shits."

"What?"

"What goes in, must come out. He who eats fire, shits fire. Didn't all those chilies get to you?"

"You had a problem with the hot stuff?"

"Problem ain't the word. Torture is the word. But I think it's all out of me. I guess that green chili chop suey is still taking revenge on the Wizard."

After a few minutes Gadgets reappeared. Mud covered his shoes and pants. He paused before getting in the van, standing in the monsoon rain, letting the water shower down on him, washing away the slimy black mud. Clean, but thoroughly soaked, he got into the van.

"What is this?" Lyons said, taking a creature off Gadgets's back. "A snail? Pol, look at this thing."

Blancanales took the creature. The size of the spiral shell seemed more appropriate to the ocean. With its antennae and long, translucent foot dangling, the snail was almost as long as Blancanales's hand.

The snail repulsed Gadgets. "Get that monster out of here! Out! Before it goes into a frenzy and eats us. Ironman, check me out. Any more of those things on me?"

But Blancanales had another idea. "Lieutenant, your country should export these things to France and Quebec. They serve a certain kind of snail as hors d'oeuvres. But each one of these could be a meal."

Lieutenant Disanayake looked as if he might vomit. He stared at the snail, finally looking away. He explained his disgust. "They feed on dung... excrement. Of people, of animals. Of dogs."

"Oh." Blancanales threw the snail out the window.

"Hey," Lyons countered. "The French don't need to know that. Package the snails here and ship them to France. *Escargo grande! Très bien. Oui! Oui!*"

Blancanales laughed. "Please, Mr. Stone! Don't even try to speak French."

"We are at the place," Disanayake announced as he slowed the van. In the headlights, they saw only falling rain and flooded asphalt. Then the lieutenant cranked a hard left turn and weaved through a tunnel of foliage. Branches scraped both sides of the van. Bumping over a rutted, rain-flooded track, they continued several hundred yards, then the lieutenant downshifted and accelerated to power up a slight rise.

The high beams swept across the darkness, revealing a gray beach torn by storm chop, then illuminated a row of small houses set under coconut palms. Constructed of concrete blocks on concrete slabs, the guest houses had tile roofs and airway windows created by squares of latticework concrete blocks. Padlocks secured the plank doors.

Disanayake parked the van under the overhang of a roof. Water cascaded from the tiles in a sheet as he unlocked the guest-house door and Able Team followed him inside.

Their flashlights waved across the interior of an empty concrete box, the concrete blocks bare and unpainted. The guest house had no furniture in the one square room, no rods or drawers in the closet, and no fixtures in the adjoining bathroom. No glass or screening covered the airway windows. Gray sheets of spiderwebs hung from the undersides of the roofing tiles.

"As you can see my friends, my family did not complete the furnishing."

"Most definitely not the Intercontinental," Gadgets commented.

"Yes, true. But it can be comfortable and pleasant. The caretaker and I will make all the arrangements so that—"

Lyons cut off the lieutenant. "Only the minimum. We didn't come here to vacation."

15

Rain drummed down on the rooftop where the Englishman stood. Sheltered only by his rage and an umbrella, Richard Hansen—transnational entrepreneur, a citizen of the world loyal only to gold—looked down on the squalor of Ratnam Road.

Yellow barricades and police cars with flashing beacon lights closed the road. One line of barricades and a row of officers stood in the traffic circle near De Mel Park, one short block to the south of Hansen. Another line closed the avenue at Station Lane, the side street immediately below where he stood.

At both lines of barricades, city of Colombo police waved flashlights to direct traffic onto Rifle Street. Passing cars and buses, transporting a few workers and managers to essential services, slowed as the drivers tried to see the disturbance at the Hotel Morningstar.

The civilians saw nothing but the high slat sides and glaring headlights of Sri Lankan army troop trucks. But the trucks did not obstruct Hansen's view.

Ignoring the rain, he stood four stories above

Ratnam Road on the roof of the Thyagarajah Brothers Cinema. The theater had been abandoned by the Tamil owners after mobs burned the staff alive in the riots of 1983. Only rats occupied the gutted auditorium and offices of the concrete hulk. Hansen watched the Morningstar and raged.

Police carried the canvas-wrapped corpses of the Koreans from the hotel and stacked them in the back of an army transport. Other police carried weapons to a police van.

The attack on the Americans had failed. The Americans had fled and only corpses remained. To be removed by the bumbling police of this decaying city.

The Americans must die. Their continued existence threatened his gold. If he succeeded in transferring the freight container concealing the argon ion laser and the mainframe computer that directed the ultraprecise laser, he received one million U.S. dollars in gold.

At three hundred fifty dollars to the Kruggerand, that came to two thousand, eight hundred fifty-seven coins of .995 fine gold.

At one ounce to the coin, almost one hundred eighty pounds or eighty-one kilograms of gold.

More than Hansen weighed. In gold. Deposited directly into his Swiss account.

How had the Americans survived?

He had arranged for the Americans to die their first night in Colombo. Die before they left the van that drove them to the Intercontinental. But they killed the Korean surveillance man, a career soldier in the peoples armed forces of the Democratic Republic of Korea, a career soldier trained since childhood to observe, to ruthlessly strike and kill, with his hands, with any weapon. And then they disappeared into the sprawling, stinking slum the Sri Lankans called the capital of their cankersore of a country.

The Colombo police or the Sri Lankan air force—Hansen did not know which gang of incompetents claimed the credit, but someone had blundered into information on the Americans. Dispatching his Korean executioners to surround the hotel, then enter and exterminate at the darkest time of the night when men slept deepest, Hansen had lost all but two of the Koreans.

Didn't the Americans sleep? How could they have escaped the assault? Without a casualty! Korean soldiers trained all their lives to infiltrate, strike, kill—and there were no Americans dead, no Americans even wounded. It was beyond belief.

Hansen realized his rage verged on despair.

What means remained to kill the Americans? His squad of Koreans was decimated; only two men remained. But what use could they be in this country? Neither man spoke English. Only one spoke Russian. They could not pursue the Americans. Could Hansen appeal to the Soviets for another group of soldiers? If he told the Soviets of the extermination of the Koreans, the Soviets would undoubtedly rush KGB operatives to Sri Lanka. The operatives would speak English. They would bring the necessary weapons and equipment for an intensive search and surveillance.

But the assembly of the Soviet unit would take time. Perhaps two days. The Soviets would arrive the same day as the freighter. Too late. That risked the destruction of the argon ion laser. One splash of gasoline by the Americans could negate months of plotting by Hansen and Verity.

What other resources could Hansen summon? Could the Soviets assemble a unit of Palestinians in Marxist Yemen? Another Korean unit? This time Hansen wanted operatives who could pass unnoticed in the dark-skinned street crowds. No one could equal the Koreans or the Soviets in murderous technique—except the Americans, Hansen cursed silently—but the Koreans, despite their dark skin, attracted attention anywhere they went here. And pale-skinned Soviets? The Americans could spot Russians a mile away.

Could his friends in the Defense Ministry provide a kill unit? Not a platoon of the jokers they called soldiers. A Sinhalese commando couldn't threaten an ice-cream vendor.

What about a gang? A mob of criminals who murdered for pay? A Sinhalese gang, like the mobs who had attacked the hundreds of Tamil shops and homes in Colombo, Matale and Kandy.

Hansen had heard the stories. Like the story of the Tamil family in the taxicab. Stopped by a mob on Galle Face Road, the taxi pelted with bottles of gasoline, the family screaming inside the burning taxi, clawing at the windows, the father trying to push a child through a window to escape. And the *goombas* of the mob, the slum criminals, darting into the flames and hacking with their knives and swords, hacking away the child's head, the father's hands, the beseeching hands of the mother, the mutilated family screaming in the flames. . . .

In the nights of chaos and looting and crazed murder, that atrocity had been repeated hundreds of times.

Hansen wanted *goombas*. He would call the under secretary and recruit an entire prison. A hundred of them, no, a thousand to search the island for the Americans. Killers who spoke the language, who knew the people, who could hunt for the strangers who were hiding somewhere. And when the *goombas* found the Americans? What if the Americans killed ten, twenty, fifty of the criminals? Hansen would pay the men who finally killed the Americans—say, a hundred American dollars. Each. If they proved they shared in the kill, they would share in reward.

Bring an American's head, get a hundred American dollars. Bring an arm, get American dollars. Bring a piece of meat with white skin on it, get a dollar.

To kill the Americans, Hansen would pay American dollars.

Hansen could afford the price of their deaths.

The Soviets were paying him in gold.

16

Poya came gray and storming. The four men slept through the first hours of the day, then woke to an afternoon of intermittent sunlight and rain. Winds drove squawls across the vast silver belly of Wattala Bay, whitecapping the water, sending storm chop to tear at the beach. The shorebreak churned the sand, the waves gray even when the overhead sun appeared between passing bands of monsoon clouds.

The guest house furnished by the caretaker provided pans and propane for cooking, but no food. With a plastic shopping bag stenciled with the Marlboro man, the lieutenant and Blancanales started to the nearest village, Hendala.

"Our walking will not be for nothing, I assure you," Disanayake said. "Some gracious soul will take pity on us travelers and consent to sell us a few things, despite the holiday of our Lord Buddha."

"Yeah, pity for the travelers," Lyons added, "who come with our Lord Dollars of the United States."

As they walked away, Lyons snapped his fingers to get Blancanales's attention. Using a gesture he learned in Mexico, Lyons pulled down the corner of his right eye for an instant, then pointed at Disanayake, meaning "Watch him closely." Blancanales understood.

Gadgets and Lyons remained at the Disanayake Palm Beach Resort, Ltd. Lounging in swim trunks and jogging shoes, they cleaned their weapons and checked their gear for shipping damage or mildew. Gadgets triple-tested his bandolier of rechargeable nicad AA batteries, then scanned the electromagnetic spectrum with his various radios, searching for entertainment. Lyons cleaned his auto-Colt, polishing the feed ramp with a bit of cotton cloth.

Finally Gadgets gave up on the radios and played his one cassette, the tape of traditional dance music from the central mountainous province of Kandy. The horns and drums and strange voices fascinated him. The music did not fascinate Lyons, however, and Gadgets reluctantly agreed to put on his headphones. But in the silence of the concrete-block guest house, the only sounds the occasional pattering of rain on the roof tiles, Lyons still heard the incomprehensible Sinhalese voices.

"Play it loud, Wizard. I'm gone."

Lyons ran on the beach, the intermittent monsoon downpours cooling him. As he weaved along the glistening band of sand firmed by the shorebreak, waves splashed his legs with saltwater even warmer than the tropical afternoon. He let the peace and beauty of the beach cleanse his mind. Forgetting the previous night and the previous years, his perceptions became his consciousness: the gray horizon of ocean, the dome of storm, the somber green of lush palm groves, the sounds of breaking waves and wind-rattled palm fronds.

Yet he did not run aimlessly. A mile to the north, he reversed direction and ran back, surprising a group of children who had seen him only moments before. He passed the row of guest houses and continued for another mile.

There, the beach ended on the shoals and sandbars of the Kelani River. Then he ran back again. He would not leave his partner without backup. He continued his back-and-forth laps, never more than a few minutes from the guest houses, amusing the watching children who could not understand why the foreigner ran nowhere, again and again.

Hours later, Disanayake and Blancanales returned with groceries, and as the day went dark with another onslaught of rain, the group of men cooked fish on the caretaker's stove.

"No pepper on mine," Gadgets told Blancanales.

"Second the motion," Lyons agreed. He sliced bananas and papayas with a double-edged fighting knife to make a fruit salad. "No red pepper, no green peppers, no curry, nothing. Another dose like last night and I'll be on an intravenous diet. For life."

"We got these potatoes," Blancanales said, holding up a can of peeled, white potatoes. "Can't get any blander than these. They're imported from England."

Gadgets took the can. "Just what my gut needs. Remember that time we were in England? Can't remember what we ate."

Rice bubbled in a pot. Lyons grimaced. "White rice. Smells moldy. Or like it's spiced with rat shit."

Blancanales interrupted him. "Quit it, Mr. Stone. I asked for brown rice. It doesn't exist here."

"Remember that time in going south from Yaquiland in the helicopter? Tortillas—real corn tortillas, carnitas, Dos Equis, avocados, green chilies that didn't rip a hole in your gut, celantro? And then zapotes? And banana liquidos in Mexico City? How about that mango sherbet mixed with nuts and chocolate—"

"Stop it!" Blancanales shouted. He pointed to one of the bags. "I got a few liters of beer. Stout. Open up a bottle and pass it around."

Finding the dark brown bottle, Lyons pried off the cap and took a gulp. The beer exploded from his face, spraying the wall with foam. His face twisted into a mask of disgust.

"This is foul! This is. . . beyond belief!" he exclaimed.

"But that is Elephant House brand, Mr. Stone," Disanayake said in defense. "The finest in Sri Lanka! It is superb. I have many Christian friends who enjoy stout often. It is, you understand, contrary to the principles of the Eighthfold Path for a Buddhist to imbibe alcohol, very improper—"

Lyons went to the window and spat. "Elephant House brand? I think I know what the elephants contribute to the brew."

"Can't be that bad. . ." Gadgets said as he reached for the bottle.

"Don't!" Lyons warned.

Gadgets drank. And gagged. He went to the window and spewed the beer outside. "It is that bad. Tastes like some kind of puke peanut brew."

"The elephants. They feed them peanuts. Problem is, a few more days in this box and I think I'll be drinking it."

"No way!" Gadgets poured the contents of the bottle out the window. "I say we make a run into Colombo tomorrow. Disanayake, is there someplace we can buy imported beer?"

"I have no doubt you could purchase whatever you desire in the shops near the embassies, though it will be very expensive."

"Great. And I need throwaway batteries. Don't want to run down my nicads listening to music. And I want some funky cassettes—"

"And American food," Lyons added.

Blancanales listed his supplies. "Magazines. Books. A kerosene lantern to read by. And window screening to keep the mosquitoes out."

"Oh, yeah," Gadgets agreed. "Amusements. Necessities. Maybe we got Koreans looking to hit us, but this boredom is most definitely serious. Tomorrow, Colombo!"

17

"Without a doubt," Richard Hansen declared. He clasped his slender white hands together, then released the grip and caressed one hand with the other. "They are the scum of the earth. Living filth."

Under secretary Selvakumar laughed. "But they are useful. We exploit their talents in measures against the Tamils. And pay them only in rupees. For dollars, I am sure they would assault even America!"

The Englishman and the Sri Lankan watched the prisoners crowding into freight trucks. At the tailgates, plainclothesmen from the Central Investigative Bureau distributed hundreds of wallet-size cards.

Each card held a black-and-white composite photo showing the faces of the three Americans.

"And if after the agents are dead," Selvakumar explained, "and any Americans should happen to see one of those cards, if they suspect that the ministry somehow participated in the betrayal and murder of the agents, we will explain that the Americans had disappeared, and that we felt obligated to find them. It was our duty."

Laughing together, they watched the first truck accelerate away from the compound.

Throughout the day, technicians of the CIB and clerks of the Defense Ministry, working under the direct supervision of Selvakumar, had organized the mass search for the Americans. The technicians took the "top secret" folder furnished by the United States government and prepared for the mass distribution of the photos and physical descriptions: rephotographing the full-face identification cards and translating the English to Sinhalese, the CIB technicians printed a thousand cards with the photos on one side, the names and descriptions of the Americans on the other.

The Defense Ministry orchestrated the logistics of the manhunt, identifying trusted detainees in the prisons of several cities for employment in the search, scheduling truck transportation to Colombo, providing offices and telephones for the plainclothes operatives who would manage the criminals. And the purchase of hundreds of knives.

Newly installed computers made the large-scale coordination possible. The Sri Lankan government had bought the data processors with funds donated by the United Nations' Educational, Scientific and Cultural Organization to study the interrelationship of airborne industrial pollution and violence in the populace. However, an officer of UNESCO declared the study unnecessary after the Soviet Union's scientists proved that wind-carried pollution from the United States and Western Europe created capitalistic delusions over the entire globe.

The Defense Ministry then appropriated the computers for the Office of National Reconciliation, which directed the covert war of extermination against the Tamil, Islamic and Christian minorities of Sri Lanka.

Eighteen hours after his desperate appeal, Hansen flew to the Northern Province with Under Secretary Selvakumar to observe the mobilization of the *goombas* of Kent Farm, a minimum-security institution that had operated at one time as a rehabilitation center.

As the light plane circled to land, Hansen viewed the clusters of houses set in rice fields. He could not believe he was looking at a prison. Selvakumar explained the history of the institution.

Created by the well-meaning dictate of the president, Kent Farm provided a peaceful community for violent and repeat felons who had served their prison terms. There, the ex-criminals lived with their families and demonstrated their reformation before returning to freedom.

However, during the disturbances of 1983, mobs of prisoners surged from Kent Farm to attack the Tamil communities of the province. The reformed felons looted, burned, raped and murdered for a week. The police cheered the rampaging gangs on to ever-increasing destruction, until one gang, pursuing a crowd of fleeing Tamils, encountered a reaper who would run no more. The Tamil rice farmer charged the gang with his two-handed scythe, slashing and hacking, inspiring the other young men and women of his community to turn against the predators. Panicked, the gangs fled back to the safety of Kent Farm.

Selvakumar told the story without the pro forma propaganda of Tamil Communist insurgency or declarations of valiant Sinhalese courage heard in every public statement by government officials. Though he lied to his country's citizens when he spoke for the radio or newspapers, he did not lie to Hansen. The two men shared a goal—gold and U.S. dollars. Hansen demanded accurate information in return for his payments. Therefore, Selvakumar spoke the truth.

The Tamils did not forget the crimes of August, 1983. In November, 1984, armed with bottles filled with gasoline—the preferred weapon of the Sinhalese, Selvakumar noted—and a few rifles and shotguns, the Hindu and Christian communities devastated Kent Farm.

The Defense Ministry refused to abandon the strategic location. Removing the families of the convicts, the Sri Lankan army surrounded the farm with barbed wire and garrisoned soldiers there to protect the Sinhalese felons. The army justified the investment by employing the felons as paramilitary police to roam the countryside and terrorize Tamils. In a few months, the armed and trained gangsters had driven out the populace and created a "pacified" wasteland.

Tonight, Selvakumar supervised the mobilization and transportation of the gangs to another area of operations, Colombo.

The assignment: kill three Americans.

"Very good.... Shall we return?" Hansen asked the under secretary. "I hope to have a few hours' rest tonight. Last night was very difficult."

"Fear not and sleep well, my English friend. Tomorrow, your trouble with the Americans shall end."

18

Easing the van through the crowds of saronged Asians, Lieutenant Disanayake tapped the horn every few seconds. An hour before, they had switched license plates with a wrecked car in Wattala. Now the three Americans in the stolen van looked out on the old commercial district of Colombo, the Pettah.

Shops and vendors lined the street. Inside the shops, merchants sat behind counters. Some wore the conservative shirts and white skullcaps of Islam, others the loud sport shirts of the Sinhalese. Vendors did business on the sidewalks, their goods displayed against the walls and on plastic sheets, forcing the passersby to walk in the street.

When the street cleared, the lieutenant accelerated, splashing through the mud and trash of the rutted street. Then another knot of foot traffic, surging around displays of combs or bananas or umbrellas, forced him to an idling roll. A small man in a loin cloth, pushing a cart loaded with bags of rice, brought the van to a complete stop. Disanayake leaned on the horn. The cart man did not even glance at the van as Disanayake lurched into motion again.

The smells of the street hit in waves. Rotting debris, diesel smoke from trucks and buses, charcoal smoke from cook shops, human odors from the alley latrines combined with the heat and humidity to create a miasma threatening to choke, to physically overwhelm the Americans.

Sweat beaded and streamed down Lyons's face. Even though he wore sunglasses, the white glare of the sky made him squint as he watched the passing shops and crowds. His lips twitched with a sneer. He turned to his partners in the back seat of the minivan. "Wizard, Pol. I volunteer to stay with the gear and monitor the receiver. You two can play tourist. Just don't forget the food I want. That food is crucial."

"All right, the gentleman's offer is most definitely accepted," Gadgets replied. "It's my turn to check out the Casbah."

"I'll come back," Blancanales offered. "So you can walk around. It's not often we get free time in Asia."

Lyons laughed once, sneering. "Who wants it? I didn't come here to play tourist and now that I'm here, forget it."

Blancanales gestured at the commercial chaos. "This marketplace is ancient. Americans talk about free enterprise. But here, free enterprise was a custom thousands of years old before the Europeans invented money."

"*Sí, Professor Pol.* I'll stay in the truck," Lyons said in acknowledgment.

"But Mr. Stone!" Disanayake interrupted. "As

your friend so eloquently stated, this is the scenic and historical Pettah, which means, literally 'outside the fort.' If it is in Sri Lanka, you can find it here.''

"*¡La ciudad de caca!*" Lyons shouted.

The lieutenant looked confused. Gadgets laughed. Blancanales closed his right fist and tapped Lyons on the side of the head.

"Quit it."

"Mr. Stone, you must have misheard me in all the noise and clamor. The name is Pettah, not Kaka.''

Looking at Gadgets, Lyons drew a long breath through his nose and choked dramatically. "I know the truth, kid. Park this truck. I'll watch it and our gear.''

"Rest assured, Mr. Stone, there is no theft here. Absolutely none. You can walk and enjoy the sights with your friends. Your equipment will be perfectly—''

"Yeah? Absolutely? You positive?''

"Yes, Mr. Stone,'' Disanayake said as he eased the van through a slow right turn and parked in an alley. "Most certainly.''

Sri Lankans glanced in at the foreigners and smiled as they passed. The men and boys also glanced at the contents of the cargo area behind the seats. Lyons noted their glances at the two shipping trunks in the back. As Disanayake opened his door to step out, Lyons caught his arm and pulled him back.

"You give me your word? You take responsibility?''

"Yes, yes! My word!"

Lyons leaned close to the young man. Disanayake flinched from the hard-faced American. But Lyons gripped his arm. "You bet your life?"

"What do you mean? Bet... wager my life?"

"You said 'absolutely.' Once upon a time, in Japan, if a soldier gave his word that something 'absolutely' would be done, and he did fail, he killed himself. Out of shame. Let me ask you again, do you 'absolutely' guarantee—"

"But this is not Japan!"

"If we walk away and our equipment is stolen, will you—"

Blancanales punched Lyons in the shoulder. It sounded as though he'd punched stone. "Quit it. He's just a kid."

But Lyons did not look away from Disanayake. "Stay out of it, Pol. I'm always hearing this lieutenant's Brit talk and I want to know if he listens to what he says. Lieutenant, if we walk away from the truck and our equipment's stolen, will you apologize by putting a bullet through your brain?"

Grabbing Lyons's wrist, Blancanales tried to break the grip on Disanayake. Lyons did not release the young soldier.

"But... but Mr. Stone. You your very self, you stole this van! Is that why you so fear theft?"

Lyons laughed again in his strange way, a single brutal sneering sound without humor or compassion. "So it ain't so absolute. On your way, Lieutenant Srilanalackie." He gave the young man a slight but jarring shove as he released his arm.

"Disanayake," the lieutenant corrected, then got out of the van, rubbing his arm.

Blancanales hissed with anger. "What is with you? What was that all about?"

"I don't trust him. He could be more dangerous than those Koreans. So you watch him closely. Don't let him out of your sight."

"It's not like you're such a fun guy," Gadgets commented. "Not like he'd want to hang out and jive and laugh with you."

Lyons laughed, and Gadgets continued, "But you got it straight. He's always trying to give us the split. But do not fear, my dear Mr. Stone. Him and me are going to be sweat to sweat. He pulls a fade, we're in motion, no doubt about it."

"If he fades," Lyons said in his partner's idiom, "we fade but quick."

"And the radio," Gadgets said, pointing to one of the equipment trunks. "If the ship comes in, the unit will alert you and simultaneously record it. Just buzz us so we know to get back."

With a salute, Gadgets followed Blancanales and the lieutenant into the crowds. Lyons slid behind the steering wheel. Touching the dangling ignition wires together, he started the engine and put the van in gear. He backed up, then eased forward again, putting the side of the van within inches of the building. He rolled down the window and sprawled sideways on the seat, the back of his head against the concrete of the wall, the open window providing cross ventilation.

He kept one hand under his folded sports coat,

resting on the grip of his auto-Colt. Behind him, the Colt Python he wore in a hidden holster cut into the small of his back.

Watching the passing Asians, Lyons waited, sweating.

19

Music blared from a hundred stereo speakers. Every other booth on Front Street seemed to offer cassettes and stereos. And the merchants advertised their wares by turning up the volume.

Gadgets continued past glass walls of watches and Jacksons' T-shirts. He carried a burlap bag heavy with imported food and beer and hardware over his shoulder. He slowed at the displays of tapes, reading cassette titles and glancing at promo posters until he stopped at a wall of speakers blasting out punk-rock wails.

The merchant behind the counter looked at the foreigner standing outside, who sweated in slacks and tropical-weight sports coat. After estimating age and nationality of the prospective customer, the merchant rejected the punk tape and played the Beatles. The merchant smiled, motioning for Gadgets to enter. When Gadgets stayed outside, the merchant punched the tape deck's Reject key and jammed in a New York-produced ska band.

Ska rhythm got him. Gadgets passed the gunnysack to Blancanales and stepped inside.

The Front Street merchants did not sell from shops. Their counters and displays and floor-to-ceiling racks occupied shacks measuring no more than three yards square. Gadgets scanned the shelves by standing in the center and turning in a circle, speed-reading the vivid jackets of the cassettes, seeing products by all the known stars of the world: the Beach Boys, Otis Redding, Jimmy Cliff, Abba, the Beatles, jazz groups, disco divas, groups with names in scarlet Arabic and ideograms and black-and-white Cyrillic lettering.

He, Blancanales and Disanayake had already spent all their rupees on necessities for the beach houses. Now Gadgets wanted cassettes. But he had no rupees. Desperate, he opened the velcro-sealed inner pocket of his sports coat. Peeling off a sweat-soaked hundred-dollar bill, he showed it to the shopkeeper.

The middle-aged man glanced at the American bill, then called out in fluid, musical Arabic. Someone in another shop answered. Gadgets called out to the lieutenant, "Disanayake! Come translate!"

"That is unnecessary, sir." The merchant spoke perfect international English. "The Bank of Ceylon rate is 29.75 rupees to the U.S. dollar. I offer you thirty even."

Gadgets considered the rate. He knew nothing about the official rate of exchange versus the street price for dollars. But he knew countries at war needed dollars for weapons and ammunition. And the citizens of the country would be exchanging their country's currency for international currencies: dollars, pounds, deutsche marks, francs, gold.

The merchant understood his hesitation. "Thirty point one zero rupees, sir."

"How much are the cassettes?"

"Most are thirty-five rupees. Unless they are double album sets. Not much more than a dollar. A very good deal."

"A dollar each. And I take my change in rupees at thirty-one to the dollar."

"How many cassettes?"

"I want them all!" Gadgets laughed. "But...I won't spend more than one hundred dollars."

"Oh, you are a music freak."

"Yeah! Gotta have it! That one, that one, that one, that one— I want everything I see!"

The merchant smiled, showing gold-edged teeth. "If you buy fifty, I will sell at one dollar each. If you buy fifty, I will make your change at the rate of 30.50 to the dollar."

"You got it! You got some shopping bags?"

In front of the booth, Blancanales stood in the shadow of the shop's awning, a gunnysack in each hand. The maddening chaos of sounds—the blaring cassettes, the voices, the shrieking of steel on stone from a sidewalk knife sharpening wheel—forced him to fix his awareness on visual perception only. He watched the hundreds of passing shoppers, looking for any unusual action—a professional glance, anyone walking past repeatedly, a hand on a concealed weapon.

Or a Korean face.

But everyone on the street seemed to be in motion. Shoppers went from booth to booth. Porters carried loads. Taxi drivers polished their cabs. Only a group of ragged men in filthy clothes idled. They crowded around the man who rhythmically pedaled the grinding wheel, a bicycle chain and gear system spinning the heavy stone wheel as he held a blade to the grindstone. The man stopped pedaling to show a short-bladed knife to one of the waiting men—laborers, mechanics?—who touched the blade's edge, then passed it back to the grinder. The shriek of steel on stone cut through all the other sounds of Front Street.

Blancanales simultaneously watched Lieutenant Disanayake. He did not want his liaison man to slip away and perhaps, unintentionally or otherwise, compromise the mission. Able Team only had to wait another day or two for the ship. Then they could do their job.

A passing Sinhalese looked at Blancanales, then looked down. The man looked again. Blancanales saw one eye with a pupil, the other eye squinted, permanently, over the cloudy white ball of a blind eye. Scars marked the man's face. The one eye looked from Blancanales to something the man held in his hand.

A card. Blancanales saw midday glare flash off the glossy surface of...a black-and-white print. The one print framed three heads, like the photo strip from a department-store photo machine.

The man moved away. Blancanales watched him. The one-eyed Sinhalese wore an oily sarong and a filthy shirt. A new black nylon belt, the nylon glistening, the brass web-style belt buckle flashing, cinched his sarong.

The red plastic handle of a knife stuck out of his belt.

No, not a knife. The off-red phenolic plastic and heavy hilt, the top half covered with a lamination of black rubber, identified the knife as a bayonet. From a Kalashnikov.

Blancanales watched the Sinhalese dodge through the crowd. The one-eyed man stopped at the group of men standing around the knife sharpener. He talked with the men. A second man, who also had a red-handled bayonet in his belt, looked across the street to Blancanales, then looked away.

The one-eyed man drew out his bayonet and held it out to the grinder, but the man shook his head and held up the job in his hands—a red-handled Kalashnikov bayonet.

To Blancanales it appeared that all the men in the group had Kalashnikov bayonets. The grinder had a line of ragged, scarred, murderous-looking Sinhalese men waiting to have their weapons sharpened. Last in line, the one-eyed Sinhalese took a wide file from the grinder's workbench and frantically tried to sharpen his bayonet. From time to time, he looked up at Blancanales.

"Wizard!" Blancanales heard his voice crack. He swallowed and tried again. "Wizard... Wizard! Get ready to move. I think... *talvez tenemos una problema. Muchas problemas con cuchillos.*"

"What?"

"Stay in there! Get the Ironman on your radio. Tell him there're street thugs out here with what looks like photos of three Americans."

"Street thugs, Mr. Pol?" Lieutenant Disanayake stared around. "There! How true. *Goombas!* Shall I go for a policeman?"

"Stay with me. Whatever happens, Disanayake, stay close. Remember, they'll want you dead, too. Wizard, tell him they've got bayonets from AKs, and that they're sharpening the bayonets and looking at me."

"Oh, shit . . . tell me you're jiving!"

"Don't come out. Don't let them see both of us until you're ready to move fast and hard."

"Doing it!" Gadgets shoved a wad of brilliant-colored Sri Lankan bank notes into a plastic shopping bag heavy with fifty-seven cassette tapes. Grabbing another bag from the merchant, Gadgets double-bagged the cassettes. He worked fast, using the merchant's package twine to make carrying straps for the bag. He now had a back-pack, and he slipped his arms through the loops of twine. A final loop of twine went around his body to hold the bag tight. Then he took out his hand radio.

"Wizard calling the Ironman."

"You done? You got some deli food?"

"Politician spotted some dudes with make-sheets on three tourists we all know and love."

"Make-sheets?"

"That's what he thinks. And—" Gadgets saw

the merchant studying the hand radio *"—y ellos tenien cuchillos. Talvez ellos quieran a cortar nosotros."*

"Got it. Where are you? I'll get the truck in motion."

"Forget it. You couldn't get through the crowds. We'll make a sprint. You have the engine running."

"Load and lock, over."

Gadgets pocketed his radio. He jerked his shoulders to test the twine holding the cassettes to his back, then called out, "Wizard in the door! Give me the green light!"

Reaching into the shop, Blancanales passed back one of the woven plastic gunnysacks. Gadgets glanced inside: cans of foreign foods, bottles of imported beer, a coil of rope, a box of heavy nails for the guest-house walls. But he didn't see the hammer. He wanted that hammer. With his free hand he reached in and confirmed the hammer on his Beretta. Cocked and locked. His thumb touched the snap closure. Secure.

The word came from Blancanales. "Follow me!"

Leaving the booth in a run, the cassettes bouncing and clattering, the heavy bag staggering him, Gadgets followed one step behind Blancanales and Disanayake. He saw the lieutenant looking around, confused, apologizing in Sinhalese to the people Blancanales shoved aside. But Disanayake saw Gadgets charging up behind him and he kept a fast pace between the Americans.

A street thug left the midday shadow of a shop. Gadgets saw a one-eyed man vectoring on Blancanales. A bayonet appeared.

Swinging the gunnysack with his left hand, Blancanales knocked the man's knife-hand aside.

Then Gadgets saw the claw hammer stop in the thug's skull. Blancanales did not break stride as he whirled, jerking the claws of the hammer free from the blood-fountaining skull, then continuing forward through the screams and shouts of the crowd.

A shape flashed at Gadgets's side. He felt the blade.

Then another thug attacked.

20

Lyons jerked back the actuator of the Konzak Assault Shotgun.

Designed and handcrafted by the Stony Man weapons master, Andrzej Konzaki, the assault shotgun looked like a telescoping-stock Colt commando rifle, but heavier, larger. The Konzak fired 12-gauge shells in semiauto and 3-shot burst modes from a 10-round box magazine. Konzaki, dead more than a year now, had incorporated elements of designs by Stoner and Atchisson. The modern concepts of Stoner, who had created the Armalite weapon system, showed in the hand-contoured pistol grip, the thumb-lever safety, the receiver and the bolt lock. Konzaki had then integrated the pragmatism of the ultraheavy—more than three pounds—bolt of Atchisson Assault Shotgun. Only the bolt made the weapon function.

Though heavy, weighing in excess of twelve pounds loaded, the selective-fire weapon had the capability of reversing an ambush, of shocking defenders, of absolutely wasting opposition with overwhelming firepower. Known affectionately as the "Lyons Crowd Killing Device," the shotgun's rate of fire emptied the 10-cartridge box magazine in less than two seconds.

Each of the hand-loaded, vacuum-forced aluminum 12-gauge shells contained fifty projectiles, a mixture of double-ought and number two spent-uranium balls, electroplated with chromium.

In less than two seconds, the assault shotgun could spray five hundred projectiles traveling twelve hundred feet per second.

Revving the engine of the van, the Konzak heavy across his thighs, Lyons looked out at the Pettah street, crowded with Asian bodies, and his loathing suddenly peaked in one seething moment of hatred. He wanted to point and spray, rip them, kill them all. Start an Asian war of extermination right now, right here.

Then the wave of nausea and loathing passed. Lyons laughed at his own hatred. In this long minute of waiting, of not knowing if his partners would survive, his imagination had gone berserk as he remembered Konzaki and his achievements. Thinking of the living and the dead, he waited with Konzaki's legacy ready, an antiterrorist stun-shock grenade only a reach away. He watched for his partners and revved the engine.

The combined height of the sidewalk and the van, now half out of the alley, allowed him to look over the heads of the Sinhalese crowd. In the direction of Front Street, he saw only bobbing heads and swirling gray smoke. Plastic awnings over street stalls blocked his view of the sidewalks.

Heads turned. Lyons had not heard the noise,

but the crowds had reacted. A block away, he saw a street stall collapse. Grabbing his hand radio, he keyed the transmit button again and again.

No answer.

He couldn't wait here. No matter what Gadgets had told him, Lyons could not wait while an unknown number of street thugs attacked his partners.

Throwing the van into gear, he accelerated, lurching to a stop when he came to two Sinhalese men in English-style suits pointing at a page in an account book. They stood in the middle of the street arguing. Lyons leaned on the horn and shoved them with the bumper.

One of the men shouted into the windshield, his dark face and false teeth like a strange fish against aquarium glass. Lyons screamed back and pressed down the accelerator slightly. The other Sinhalese leaned into the side window.

"I say! You rotter! You are violating the law!" he shouted.

"Shit on the law!"

The man saw the weapons on the front seat and screamed, running backward and waving his hands. A hundred faces looked at Lyons.

Closing his fist around the pistol grip of the Konzak, Lyons thumbed down the fire selector one click to semiauto and jammed the fourteen-inch barrel out the window. He pointed at the sky and fired a round.

Panic. Legs appeared under sarongs as men ran everywhere, vendors scrambled, shop doors slammed. Lyons knew what he had to do. Flipping up the Konzak's safety, he propped the shotgun against his right side, the barrel protruding menacingly out the window.

He jerked the pin from the stun-shock and pitched the grenade twenty yards ahead of the van.

Mud and trash sprayed as the boom reverberated in the narrow street. The deafening explosion had cleared the pavement, but it did not stop the attack of thugs.

At the end of the block, Lyons saw Blancanales bring down a hammer on a knife hand, the midday glare glittering on steel as the blade spun to the paving stones. But other knives flashed in arcs. A thug's slash scored on Gadgets.

Lyons stood on the accelerator, the transmission whining in low gear, the van fishtailing through the slime. The scene ahead of him expanded, zooming in perspective as he struggled to hold the van's front end on line.

Using gunnysacks as shields and flails, Blancanales and Gadgets fought along the right-hand side of the street, keeping their right sides to the clutter of booths and displays. This forced the thugs to attack across the open street. When a thug tried to attack through the booths, the Americans avoided him by dodging and advancing, stepping into the street to meet thrusts, then retreating diagonally. But they always gained distance in their retreat toward the van.

Even Disanayake fought, using the stout pole of some vendor's awning to thrust and parry in classic bayonet style. Jabbing a thug, he then swung the other end around to strike, then met the next attack. He lacked the strength or technique to injure, but finally, finally, Lyons saw the Sri Lankan acting like a soldier.

Gadgets swung a gunnysack with both hands. He connected with a head and white foam exploded from the sack. Three thugs staggered back. They looked away from their targets too late to see the van speeding at them.

Impact and the brakes threw Lyons against the steering wheel. A head came through the windshield, the mouth screaming, spraying blood. Lyons gripped the steering wheel with his right arm and slammed his left elbow into the throat once, stopping the scream in a choke of collapsed cartilage, twice, driving the head back through the glass.

With no time to extend the Konzak's tube stock, Lyons swung out of the van with the assault shotgun held tight against his body, the strength of his right arm securing the stock high against his ribs, his left hand gripping the black plastic of the forestock to hold the muzzle down as he fired. He did not aim with the sights.

Pointing, pivoting his body to aim the weapon, he fired single shots, each blast killing or maiming.

An onrushing thug raised a knife, and a blast ripped a yawning wound through his chest, throwing him back into the falling body of a disemboweled thug killed by the same blast. Another thug, hit by the van, crabbed across the stones to his knife.

Lyons turned and fired once, missing the crawling man's torso but ripping away both arms. The hood fell on his face and screamed into the filth.

Behind Gadgets, a man climbed through the wreckage of a display of plastic jewelry and purses and acrylic picture frames. Lyons pointed the short barrel of the Konzak but did not fire. Several steps past the thug, the vendors and shoppers crouched against the walls of the shops, crying and shouting in panic.

"Wizard!"

But the Able Team electronics specialist had already turned, not swinging the gunnysack, but responding with escalating technology. At point-blank range, he triggered a 3-round burst from his silenced Beretta, the low-velocity 9mm bullets punching a line of three red dots in the oil-and-filth pattern of the thug's once-white shirt.

The silenced but underpowered bullets did not stop the man with the knife. He continued in his leap, and as Gadgets sidestepped, the man staggered across the street and Lyons met him, jamming the muzzle of the Konzak down into the thug's gut, firing a contact blast through his body at a forty-five-degree angle.

Blood sprayed Lyons's face as the *goomba*'s body exploded. But Lyons did not stop to wipe off the splash of gore. Spinning, he felt a knife sear his left shoulder and he fired again. The knife caught the cloth of his jacket, and a hand clawed at him as the rotten mouth opened and screamed. The man fell, a leg at right angles to his body, ripped away except for ligaments and a rag of polyester.

Turning, Lyons scanned the street, looking for more knifemen. He heard the slap of bullets striking flesh. Two steps away, Gadgets tracked targets over the sights of his Beretta.

"Move!" Lyons shouted. "Time to move! In the truck, Wizard!"

A shout came from Disanayake. Struggling with thugs, he kicked and screamed as two held the pole while another slashed at him with a blade. A fourth thug jumped on Disanayake's back, dragging him back. The group staggered into the tangle of booths and hanging plastic and poles.

"In the van!" Lyons shouted again, even as he charged to rescue the lieutenant, hurdling a corpse, splashing through mud, crashing into the back of a thug.

The man turned with a knife and Lyons whipped around the welded steel butt of the tube stock, smashing the man's right temple, the steel gouging away his right eye as Lyons drove the butt down into the gasping man's throat and shoved him away.

Under a tangle of filthy bodies and arms waving knives, Disanayake punched at his attackers.

Lyons got extreme. Crouching for an instant, he levered the Konzak's muzzle under two men with knives and fired, throwing the bodies aside like a power shovel. He slammed the barrel to the other side, knocking a thug over, firing point-blank into the *goomba's* chest. The lieutenant drove a knife straight up into the face of the last attacker.

Disanayake saw Lyons and drew back his arm to slash, but stopped. "Mr. Stone!"

"Up and out, Lieutenant! We won! Time to retreat." Grabbing Disanayake by his left arm, Lyons jerked him to his feet and dragged him through the corpses and blood of the street.

A last thug rushed the van, reaching through the sliding door to hack at Gadgets. Blancanales, behind the steering wheel, turned and fired a burst from his Beretta, staggering the man. Lyons fired a one-handed shot, grunting with the Konzak recoil, the blast spraying the thug's guts over the side of the van.

Disanayake scrambled through the van's side door. Lyons stopped. Turning, as Blancanales gunned the engine behind him, he eyed the street.

No one attacked now. The dead and maimed lay everywhere. Groans and cries came from the dying *goombas.*

Along the buildings, from windows, from the roofs of the three-story shops, hundreds of Sri Lankans watched.

Lyons pointed the shotgun at the nearest of the crying, writhing thugs and killed the dying until the Konzak's bolt locked back.

Then he raised the empty weapon above his head and shouted out in his best Saint Patrick's Day Irish, "Death to England! Death to the imitation-English of the world! Victory to the Irish Republican Army!"

Hands jerked him into the van and tires screamed. Laughing, Lyons leaned out the door and continued shouting. "Death to the English, death to the Lackies, death to the Canadians. The queen sucks—"

"What are you talking about?" Gadgets demanded. "Shut the fuck up!"

"I want them to look for Irish terrorists. Make sense? Instead of them looking for Americans, they'll be shaking down people who—"

"Shut up!" Blancanales screamed back. "How do we get out of here? I told you to wait and now this van's all smashed up and bloody. Think we can get through a checkpoint?"

"That will be unnecessary...." Disanayake's voice quavered with delayed shock. He looked out at the blur of streets. "Turn to your right at the next— Turn right!"

Skidding sideways, the van made the turn, Blancanales whipping the wheel to avoid a truck, then a group of boys with a soccer ball. The boys stared at the blood-splashed, broken-windowed van.

"Now left! Proceed immediately across the road. Disregard the laws, disregard safety—we must cross."

Blancanales accelerated and braked and swerved, weaving through the buses and trucks like a madman—or an escaping terrorist.

"There! Do you see that street? There!"

Smashing the axles against the frame, the van hit a dip, then rocked into the air, skidding as Blancanales fought for control. He stood on the brake, coming to a tire-smoking stop in front of a crossbar gate.

"Do not stop! The gate is only wood!"

Blancanales backed up, then accelerated forward, the crossbar snapping, the van hurtling through a row of storage shacks. To the right, they saw a railroad yard. Blancanales slammed on the brakes again as they came to a drop-off.

A lake shimmered. On the other side, they saw more railway yards and warehouses.

"Dead end!" Blancanales cursed.

"No, that is not so, my friend. Look, down there! See?"

At a line of rotting docks, small boats floated motionlessly on the mirror-calm water.

Two minutes later, their weapons and equipment—and plastic bags of cassettes and beer-soaked gunnysacks filled with cans and broken glass—lay in the hold of a launch. Blancanales hotwired the ignition and the lieutenant piloted the boat through a maze of canals to the open sea, then north to the resort by the beach.

21

Blancanales worked like a tailor with a deadline. After splashing their wounds with rubbing alcohol, slapping on a daub of antibiotics, he went to work with sutures, closing up the knife wounds from the street fight.

"Could've been a whole lot worse," Gadgets commented while Blancanales stitched cuts on his left shoulder and arm. He examined a red-handled Kalashnikov bayonet. "The Kremlin doesn't make these things for knife fighting. They're for cutting wire and jamming through ribs. Look at that, Iron-man, check out that edge—"

Lyons took the blade. The bayonet had a flat, wide blade perforated with rectangular holes. A lug on the sheath slipped through the hole to create wire cutters.

Rather than tapering to a cutting edge, the blade had been machined from one side only, like a scissors's blade.

"If it was made like a knife, it wouldn't cut wire," Gadgets continued. "Look at where they tried to sharpen it."

The marks of a grindstone showed along the flat side of the blade. But the steel had resisted the grinding and remained dull.

"Someone thought these bayonets looked dangerous," Lyons said. "Someone had these bayonets and they looked dangerous and they issued them. Whoever sent the Koreans against us thought they could fall back on local assassins, but they blew it."

"Question is," Gadgets concluded, "who has a stock of AK bayonets?"

Lyons looked at Disanayake. The young lieutenant sat on the caretaker's bed, studying the stitched wounds patterning his arms and shoulders. After the half-hour boat ride north from Colombo, crusted with blood, the lieutenant had still shaken from adrenaline build up. Blancanales had prescribed a sedative painkiller.

"How do you feel, Disanayake?" Lyons asked.

"Very well, Mr. Stone."

"Say, 'I'm feelin' no pain.' "

"I'm feeling no pain."

"That's almost okay. What's your idea? Who would have boxes of bayonets in stock? Kalashnikov bayonets, to be exact."

"Would you like me to answer truthfully?"

"Talk straight," Lyons said in encouragement.

"Then I'll say it straight. The government."

"There it is," Gadgets said. "We got the Soviets and the Sri Lankans on us. Very bad scene."

"Not us," Lyons countered. "When we're done, we go home. The lieutenant stays here."

"We could get him a visa into the U.S.," Blancanales suggested.

"Or wherever. Personally," Lyons continued, "I think the lieutenant earned his money today. I move that we double his pay, in recognition of wounds received in combat, combat in which he distinguished himself as a mean man with a stick."

"Seconded!" Gadgets agreed.

Blancanales made it unanimous. "He earned a bonus."

Confused, Disanayake only nodded. Lyons started out the door of the beach house. He paused to apologize to the young man. "Sorry about the shit I gave you today."

On the front steps, Lyons faced into the setting sun. He painted his stitches with Mercurochrome from a first-aid kit. An offshore breeze stirred the palms above him and feathered the breaking waves. After the Pettah, he needed peace.

Lieutenant Disanayake, walking loose from the painkiller, sat down beside Lyons. The drug had also released his inhibitions.

"I do not understand you, Mr. Stone. Today you hated me. And today you risked your life to save me. Now you speak of more money for me and perhaps a visa to the United States. But do you still hate me?"

"I didn't hate you. I don't hate you. Really, it's not you. It's me. Sometimes I get so panicky. I try to make believe that I'm not afraid so I call it panic, and the response is nonspecific aggression. And then everyone's a target. Especially someone who talks like an Englishman. That's you. So you got the aggression. Sorry."

"But you speak English!"

"No I don't. I speak American. Not as well as Mr. Wizard, but I try."

"It sounds like English to me, Mr. Stone. Are you joking with me?"

"Say, 'Are you jiving me?'"

Disanayake hesitated. Lyons watched as the young man thought. Then, from nowhere, Disanayake tried a voice. Perhaps from a film or a soul record he had heard, from somewhere in his memory, the voice came.

"You are *jiving* me!"

"You're on your way, kid! That's a start! Just remember one thing—and this enlightenment comes straight from Mr. Wizard—whenever you hear English coming out of your mouth, that's the Empire talking. You ain't English. So why talk like one? And if you talk like an Englishman, they won't let you in the United States."

Disanayake laughed and laughed. As the sun set, he talked with Lyons, questioning the contradictory American about the United States. Lyons answered the questions and tutored the lieutenant in the idiomatic English spoken by Americans. Finally, tranquilized by sedative-painkiller, the lieutenant sprawled on the caretaker's bed and slept.

Lyons signaled for his partners to walk outside with him. Halfway to the surf, where they could watch the door of the beach house and without any possibility of the lieutenant overhearing, they discussed the possibility of the Sri Lankan betraying them.

"He thinks I'm his pal now, but that don't mean shit. He hears us talking about money and tickets to the U.S., and he says he's our friend. I say we test him."

"Hey, Ironman," Gadgets protested. "We know he wasn't in on the charge of the *goomba* brigade. We watched that boy. And I watched him get cut."

"They could have decided he was expendable. Or that street gang might have just gone berserk. This afternoon doesn't count. The gangs were searching for us, and they found us. We've got to test him before we trust him to take us into the harbor."

"How?" Blancanales asked.

"Give him the chance to make contact."

"And then?"

"We wait."

Blancanales shook his head. "No. If we give him the chance to set us up, he may or may not actually betray us. If he does call his commander, Disanayake may not be the one who then betrays us. His officer may be the one cooperating with the Soviets. Then we're on the run again, and without our liaison. And he saved us today. We wouldn't have gotten out of the city with that van."

"I know, I know. But there's been Commie double agents who killed other Commies to maintain their cover."

"The Reds don't care who dies," Gadgets added. "They just want the job done. So how we going to test him?"

"What I think is possible is this," Blancanales began. "He believes we trust him, and in fact, I do. However, when you asked him about the bayonets, he answered, 'the government.' We should play on that. He knows we suspect someone in his command. If we instruct him to report to his commander, with the intent of his commander or someone betraying us, he'll do as we say—"

"That doesn't test him," Lyons interrupted.

Blancanales continued. "We introduce a variable. We tell him we are testing his officers and we tell him to report our position. But he must not reveal one detail, because if he does, we will be trapped. If a gang comes, if soldiers come, we know an officer passed on the information to the Soviets or someone working for the Soviets. But if they come knowing the variable, we know it's Disanayake."

"Oh, yeah," Gadgets said, nodding. "I'll go for that. A triple-cross. Makes it interesting. What's the plan?"

Blancanales crouched and sketched a map in the sand.

22

Gold-plated, highlighted with details of plastic ivory, the Louis XIV-style telephone played a minuet in chime tones. Captain Wijayasiri allowed the caller to wait as he enjoyed the melody. A gift from a French transnational company that had wanted to sell solid-state telephone switching equipment to the Sri Lankan air force, the telephone provided many moments of joy to the captain.

Though nothing came of the French sales effort—the company had abandoned the effort to sell to the air force after two years of frustration and the "gifts" of ninety-three telephones—the captain thought of the venture as a success. He had profited, had he not? Did he not now listen with pleasure to the delicate notes of the delightful musical device?

Finally he lifted the receiver. Static hissed, almost drowning out the faint voice he heard. Pops and clicks punctuated the whisper. Wijayasiri shouted into the line.

"Hello! Who's there? Speak louder, please!"

"It is Lieutenant Disanayake. I have slipped away from the Americans. I have information."

"It has been days! Why have you not reported? All the men searched for you. And you have taken the Americans to none of the places of my friends."

"They kidnapped me! It is the truth."

"How could they kidnap you? You are an officer in the air force of Sri Lanka. Have they no respect for your position? Order them—"

"Captain! They are terrorists! They think nothing of killing. They are cruel and cunning. I have only now slipped away because they are drunk, debauched, celebrating after the murders today in the Pettah. Surely you know of the bombs and shooting in the Pettah."

Wijayasiri spat out a curse in Sinhalese, then returned to his correct English. "You lout! You worthless layabout! Now I know you make excuses. Several witnesses reported that those terrorists declared—they themselves declared!—that they represented the Irish Republican Army. That they cursed England. That they said an obscenity of Her Royal Highness the Queen! Irish, they were, Irish scoundrels. Of that there can be no doubt!"

"But I was there! I was in the fight, I escaped in the car. Why can you not listen?"

"You? Little Disanayake, the boy who tinkers with radios? A terrorist? I think you have been drinking arrack. Arrack! I want you to report tomorrow and explain yourself. That is what must be done, yes. You must explain yourself in person, so that I can see for myself if you are intoxicated. I believe the Americans to be a terrible influence on you."

"But I cannot leave the Americans! They will not allow me to leave. I am their prisoner."

"You can tell me of the Americans tomorrow."

"No, tonight!"

"Why tonight? It is too late to return to the office. It is against procedures."

"Captain, I must talk to someone this very night. May I call the Defense Ministry? It is they who allowed these demented foreigners into our country."

"There is a number," Wijayasiri began, "but you cannot tell them I provided the telephone number. Your dereliction of duty is an embarrassment to me. Do you realize you did not fulfill one, not one, of the obligations to patronize the establishments of my friends? I wish to be rid of you. Here is the number...."

In the public telephone booth of the Lansiyawatta post office, Disanayake carefully printed the phone number. Other Sri Lankans waiting to use the telephone pressed against the glass door. After he hung up, he pushed the door open, slipped past the shoving people and hurried out of the post office. Blancanales stood in an alcove behind the booth. He waited a moment, then followed the lieutenant into the night.

Lyons and Gadgets stood under the night shadow of a flowering silk tree. Blancanales silently followed the lieutenant. He leaned against the post-office wall, so that he also appeared to be waiting.

"So how'd it go?" Gadgets asked.

"My captain did not believe me. He told me to report to his office tomorrow. However—"

"What?" Lyons interrupted. "He didn't want information on us?"

"No jive! I tell you straight, my friends. I believe Captain Wijayasiri has washed his hands of me. Perhaps the incident has embarrassed him. But I did persuade him to give me the number of a person in the Ministry of Defense. Should I now call the ministry?"

Blancanales crossed the sidewalk and asked, "Is it the phone number of the offices or a person?"

"He said person. But the person may be in the offices—"

"Not at night," Gadgets told the lieutenant.

"The country is in a state of emergency," the lieutenant countered. "There will be workers in the offices at all hours, I believe."

"Then try it," Lyons told him.

"It will only be another few minutes." The lieutenant returned to the post-office lobby. At the window for telephones, he put down a ten-rupee note and reserved ten minutes on the public telephone. Then he stood in line as others made their calls.

"Did he speak English in there?" Lyons asked Blancanales.

"The entire conversation. He had to argue with his officer to get that phone number. I could not believe what I heard. But he didn't try to set us up."

Gadgets laughed. "Here we are, three terrorists on the run, and the lieutenant can't even inform on us. There is something wrong with this place. An Asian twilight zone."

In the telephone booth, Disanayake dialed the number. A voice answered in perfect English.

"Aybovan. Hotel Oberoi."

23

His feminine hands writhed and twisted, gripping and releasing each other, his fingers moving like knots of white snakes.

Hansen watched the contortions and knottings of his hands, fascinated. They seemed to move of their own volition.

Nerves, the Englishman thought. This absolutely must go right. The ship comes tomorrow.

In the air-conditioned comfort of a Mercedes, Patrick Hansen and Under Secretary Selvakumar raced through the countryside, the driver sounding the horn, flashing the high beams to scatter the seemingly endless lines of Sri Lankans strolling along the narrow road.

White shirts and checked sarongs, the polyester skirts of young women, the saris of older women—all flashed in the glare of the headlights, then streaked past, glowing red for an instant in the illumination of the taillights. Then the headlights of the troop trucks silhouetted the pedestrians.

The under secretary talked of a news report. "Of course, it is indeed only a rumor, but if Her Royal Highness the princess were to grace our country with a visit, even if her assuredly hectic travels limited her stay to only a few hours, it would be a wonderful gift to Sri Lanka."

"The princess?" Hansen watched the palms and rice fields float past. He tried to politely listen to the under secretary, but he thought only of killing the Americans.

"The lovely and alluring Diana, Princess of Wales. Perhaps this vicious campaign of libel and propaganda waged by the international press would relent if in the eyes of the international community, my country could be seen as the paradise it is, rather than as it is portrayed by the European and North American media. You must remember that we had high hopes for the visit of the prince many years ago, but he chose not to step from his plane. A very great disappointment to the people of Sri Lanka, who are loyal members of the Commonwealth, who very greatly need the support of the royal family in this time—"

"I'm sorry, Selvakumar, but my mind is on the action. If we do not succeed tonight, if there is another failure, it is very serious. Very, very serious."

Selvakumar smiled. He powered down the side window and flicked the butt of his Players cigarette into the humid night. "But why do you worry? Was the Pettah so serious?"

"It wasn't exactly a resounding victory, would you say? My Lord, those Yanks made mincemeat, literally made bloody mincemeat of those cutthroats."

"We cannot assume those terrorists were the

Americans. The terrorists did declare themselves to be—"

"Oh, don't let them lead you astray with the talk of Irish Republican Army! Why would there be an IRA unit in Sri Lanka, for heaven's sake?"

Flicking his gold lighter, the under secretary touched the flame to another imported cigarette. His eyes narrowed to a squint as he affected the look of an internal-security operative. "They are in league with the Tamils. It is one more conspiracy against Sri Lanka." Then he laughed, coughing smoke and waving the glowing cigarette. "It will be as you say. They were Americans. Our intelligence reports the killers as Irish, but—"

"This gang must end the matter tonight! Tonight!"

"But they will! Have we not distributed shotguns and pistols? You need only identify these fellows, that is all that should concern you now. You identify them as Americans and all your concerns end. Like that!" Selvakumar said, snapping his fingers.

The Mercedes slowed and lurched to a stop on the muddy roadside. Trees and palms overhung the car, creating a tunnel of darkness. The chauffeur spoke quickly with Selvakumar in Sinhalese.

"Now we go," the under secretary told Hansen. "The road to the resort is back there. You will spy out the Americans and then we will send in the men."

They stepped into the Asian night. Twenty yards behind them, the trucks parked. Hansen blinked into the headlights, then looked down. He used the next few seconds of light to walk around patches of mud and roadside garbage.

Darkness came suddenly. Hansen heard Selvakumar stumbling beside him and the thugs in the trucks talking and laughing. Then both men flicked on flashlights.

"Do not hesitate, my friend! You must see the men. It is the only way to resolve all doubt. We do not want to eliminate innocent tourists, now do we?"

Insects swirled around Hansen. Fireflies scratched the black with sparks of light. He felt sweat dampening his body, but not from the evening heat.

What if he identified the men as the American agents and the cutthroats killed a group of tourists who happened to be American? No matter. He would risk that. He must, of course, instruct the leader of the gang to search for weapons and spy equipment. To confirm the elimination of the threat.

What if the Americans had a sentry? What if they questioned him? He could not bear the thought of pain, the physical abuse those animals might inflict.

The Englishman dismissed those thoughts. He had photos of the American agents. But the Americans knew nothing of his role in the transshipment of the laser and computer. Too many false companies and Swiss accounts separated Patrick Hansen from the theft of the technology and the

murders of the truck drivers. No one could guess
that Hansen had played a role in any of the crimes.

If the Americans saw him and asked why he had
come to their houses, he would...he would invite
himself in for a spot of tea! In that way, he could
subtly question the agents. Wouldn't that be pleasant? Sitting across from the Yanks and feeling the
pleasure of lying to their faces, sipping their tea and
counting the minutes until he returned to the truck
with the command to kill.

Almost laughing as he followed the light splashed
onto the ground by his flashlight, Hansen followed
the under secretary into the night.

"YOU GOT PATRICK HANSEN coming down the
road," Lyons whispered into his hand radio. "I
heard him and a Srilanalackie talking. Hansen's
identifying us, the Lackie said. Before we get elimi-
nated."

Lyons watched the road from behind the absolute blackness of a bush. Blancanales's reply
came through the earphone plugged into his ear.
"Any others? Cars? Trucks?"

"They came in a limousine. I heard trucks parking; I count two by the sounds and I hear voices inside the trucks."

"That's confirmed," Gadgets interjected. "Two
trucks."

"And they're identifying us? No one else coming?"

"Only Hansen and a Lackie dressed up like a
playboy."

"I'm in motion," Blancanales told his partners. "He's got to see some Americans at the beach houses. Do you agree that this is a confirmation on the loyalty of our liaison?"

"Maybe..." Lyons admitted.

But Blancanales did not hear. He and Lieutenant Disanayake hurried through the vertical shadows of a palm grove. Waiting without flashlights for hours, they had preserved their night vision. The lights of Colombo, reflecting on the overcast sky, provided a faint gray light. They angled away from the dirt track leading from the road until they came to the sandbanks above the shorebreak. They skied down the sand, then sprinted along the beach.

Seconds later, Blancanales paused at the trail leading to the houses and placed his M-16/M-203 and bandoliers of ammunition in the darkness beside a fallen palm. Then they ran to the beach houses. Blancanales flicked on the light of the caretaker's cabin. Then he switched on the radio. He hurried on to the next cabin.

Throwing open the plank door of the unoccupied cabin, Blancanales grabbed the penlight from his shirt pocket. He switched on the light and jammed the pen into a crack in the wall. The beam shone on the far window, making the concrete-block latticework glow.

Blancanales went outside. From there, the light was clearly visible. "Lieutenant! Go in there. Move around so you make shadows on that window. Now, go, go."

A flashlight appeared in the darkness. Blancanales followed the rutted track a few steps. He glanced back and saw the lighted cabin. The radio's music and voices came loud despite the surf. Sounded like a party. And the glow in the window of the other cabin shifted every few seconds, indicating movement inside.

Strolling through the night, Blancanales went to meet the Englishman. He rehearsed his best New Jersey accent.

AN AMERICAN! Hansen's hand trembled, the flashlight shaking. His other hand, like a wandering creature, touched his lips, smoothed back his hair, tugged on the collar of his polyester safari jacket. But he could not turn back. Hansen followed as Selvakumar continued on toward the hulking American.

Hansen's heart thundered. What would the American do? Would there be a fistfight? Would he shoot Hansen? How much money should he offer the American to let him go? Should he say that Selvakumar ran the enterprise to sell American technology to the Soviets?

"You two! What do you want here?" the American demanded, his voice hard and humorless.

"Hello, my dear fellow," the under secretary called out. He put the beam of the flashlight on the face of the American.

"Get that light out of my face!"

The Puerto Rican agent. But Hansen did not see the other Americans.

Selvakumar shone the beam on the mud. "A thousand apologies. We search for my friend Mr. Pindalamatalawattelle."

"Pindala—what? There's no one here like that."

"But he told us he would be here."

Hansen studied the guest houses. He saw lights in two cabins. Music came from one. The lights and music, and the hard face of the Yank in front of them, proved the identity of the Americans. Now Hansen wanted to retreat to the safety of the Hotel Oberoi before the slaughter.

One last consideration: the information on the American agents came from the Sri Lankan liaison officer assigned to the agents. Should Hansen direct the leader of the gangs waiting in the trucks to spare the lieutenant?

And leave a possible witness?

No.

"There's only the four of us here. And none of us are called Pindalatwat. So move it! Turn around and get out of here. This is private property. Get out!"

"Certainly, certainly. We want no disturbance," Selvakumar said.

Hansen and the under secretary retraced their way along the rutted, muddy track. Neither spoke until they left the American far behind.

"What a beastly rotter!" Selvakumar cursed. "I will celebrate when I hear of his death."

"So will I, Selvakumar. So will I. Now you know why the world hates Americans."

"Late drinks at the Oberoi? While we wait for the glad news?"

"No, my friend. I fear I can't. But I will see you tomorrow, I'm sure."

The Englishman had a late-night appointment with another Sri Lankan. One with dark eyes and long, slim thighs.

"Oh, yes. Tomorrow. More equipment comes for the exhibition, does it not?"

"Yes, it is related to the exhibition."

At the road they signaled the gang leaders.

Kill the Americans.

24

"Wizard! Get a radio-pop across to me!"

"For the Mercedes? No way now...."

Seething with frustration and anger, Lyons watched the Sri Lankan official and the English techno-pirate get into the Mercedes. Lyons held his silenced Colt Government Model—his Konzak lay beside him in the mud—but he could not kill the Englishman.

Able Team's plans for the night did not include a slaughter on this country road. And it would be a slaughter if Lyons fired.

Leaving the trucks, men with shotguns and swords rushed across the road, their voices and laughter disappearing into the darkness of the narrow track running to the beach houses. Even if he and Gadgets killed twenty of the thugs in the first slash of full-auto fire, another twenty would survive. In daylight, on familiar ground, he and Gadgets could exterminate the gang that came to murder them. But in the night? Searching for men with rifles and shotguns and knives in total darkness? With civilians in the area?

No, Gadgets had the better plan. Lyons had to let the two men drive away in the Mercedes.

Watching the luxury car drive into the distance, Lyons keyed his hand radio. "Politician. The English shit's gone. You've got the gang coming to get you now."

"How many?"

"Too many. Forty, fifty. They've got rifles, long barreled shotguns, pistols. And machetes. Get out of there so they can tear up the place."

"In motion. . ."

"Wizard, what goes?"

"I'm laying cool till the *goombas* go. Looks like the drivers will stay in the cabs. This'll be too easy. Like murder."

"Want to fight fair? Join the YMCA."

"You hear me say no? In fact, here I go. Key me if any of them come back."

"Will do. Off."

Thirty yards away from Lyons, Gadgets Schwarz cinched his CAR tight against his back. With his Beretta 93-R cocked and locked in a belt holster, the black-clad Stony Man fighter crept out of the tangled brush and vines. He watched the trucks as he moved silently through the wet trash, finally freeing all of his body from the concealing undergrowth.

Gadgets paused. Flat in the mud and trash, he scanned the roadsides and the trucks. He could see nothing in the darkness across the strip of asphalt, and he heard no one walking or speaking. Faint light came through the cab window of the second truck, the glow lighting the slat benches and plank platform of the canvas-covered transport.

Rising, he took five steps to the back of the truck. He crouched and listened. Voices came from the front. Chancing another move, Gadgets took another few steps, his feet silent in the mud and leaves. He stopped at the cab of the truck.

No voices. No movement. He stood to his full height and looked inside the cab. The domelight illuminated the interior. He saw that the driver's door was open, then crept to the next truck.

The drivers talked and laughed in the cab, and Gadgets did not hesitate longer. He went back a few steps. Slowly easing his weight onto the tailgate so that the truck did not lurch and betray him, he crawled across the planks. His hands felt slime everywhere.

In the faint light from the cab of the truck, Gadgets saw the sheen of spit. Betel spit. The thugs had spit their betel juice—red as fluorescent blood, slimy with mucous, stinking of tobacco and rotting teeth—everywhere on the old planks.

The stink and the thought of the tuberculosis and whatever other diseases the *goombas* carried nauseated Gadgets, but he continued to the sheet metal of the cab.

On each side of the transport, wooden benches ran from the cab to the tailgate. Gadgets reached under the bench where it met the cab. He placed the explosive at a point directly behind the driver.

A strip of plastic pulled off the slab to expose an adhesive surface. Gadgets pushed the adhesive against the cab. Then he pushed a radio-impulse detonator into the C-4.

The charge would kill the driver and kill or maim many of the thugs in the back of the truck. But the bodies of the men around the explosion would shield the men near the tailgate. How could he kill them all?

How could he kill all these pesky Asian assassins? Gadgets wished he had brought a can of methyl isocyanate, known by its trade name of Bhopalocan.

As he listened to the Sri Lankan truck drivers talking in the cab, he found a roll of black tape in his kit. He put one wrap around an MU50G controlled-effect grenade. The tiny grenade, designed for the close-quarter combat of antiterrorist actions, had a forty-six gram charge of TNT to propel 1,400 steel balls. The reduced charge of explosive limited the one hundred percent kill diameter to ten yards.

With the safety lever secure, Gadgets tore off a length of tape and pressed the tape onto the sheet metal of the cab. The grenade hung against the slab of C-4, only the narrow plastic tape holding the grenade in place. Then he slipped out the safety lever. Though the grenade might explode simultaneously with the plastic explosive, if the blast threw the grenade any distance at all before the RDX popped, or if the fuse delayed the pop six seconds, the thousand-plus steel balls would rip the legs of the other thugs.

Worth a try, Gadgets thought. He crabbed off the platform and eased himself down to the mud. Then he waited a few seconds, listening, before continuing to the second truck.

There, he tried a more ambitious setup. He placed the C-4, then taped another MU50G in place. However, this time he separated the grenade from the C-4 with a paperback book he had found in the back of the truck. Gadgets speculated that the pulp novel might act as a buffer to the expanding gases of the exploding plastique compound, disintegrating the novel and not the grenade, creating a delay before the grenade exploded.

As he pressed the last strip of tape over the improvised charge, he heard the not-too-distant report of a shotgun.

A *goomba* shooting at shadows?

Then the earphone from his hand radio shouted the answer. "Wizard! Iron! They're on us!"

Gadgets did not waste another second on the art of killing by explosive charge. He jumped from the truck and returned to the concealment of the brush and mud. Keying his radio, he whispered, "Pol! Where are you?"

No answer came.

BLANCANALES DRAGGED Disanayake through the brush, thrashing through bushes and vines. His M-16/M-203 over-and-under assault rifle-grenade launcher caught on a branch. As Blancanales twisted free, another shotgun blast shattered the night.

Birdshot tore through the foliage, chopping leaves and wood a few yards away from the two men. Blancanales pushed Disanayake flat. The young lieutenant's lungs heaved with exertion and panic. Then more blasts tore the trees as the gang fired single-shot shotguns at the unseen men.

Flashlights swept the tangled growth. Blancanales watched the beams cross and crisscross, the glows shattered to scintillating smears by the thirty yards of bushes, vines and trees separating him from the gang. The thugs called out to one another, laughing and shouting, firing shots into the dark. A revolver popped twice, the slugs cutting through branches and leaves until they slammed into solid wood.

Blancanales whispered to Disanayake. "Stay calm. They can't shoot us unless they can see us, and they can't see us. So don't—"

"But what if they search for us?"

"They won't come in here. If they do, if they find us, I'll kill them." Then Blancanales spoke into his hand radio as the shooting continued. "Pol here, laying low while the *goombas* waste ammunition."

"What happened?" Lyons asked.

"They split up. Some of them went by the road, some of them cut through the palm groves. We ran into them and they started shooting."

"They identify you?"

"No. They're shooting at everything that moves."

"Can you get out? Or do you want us to kill some of them?"

"No. Do not—repeat, do not—deviate from the plan. The lieutenant and I will get out somehow.

Just lay low and wait. If they find me, that's different.''

A whispered laugh came from Gadgets. "Then it's their problem."

A pistol shot ripped over Blancanales. He put his face into the warm, moist earth and whispered, "You made the placement, Wizard?"

"Most definitely. Both trucks set to pop."

A fury of muzzle reports came from the direction of the beach houses. Then came the sound of breaking glass and clanging pans. Despite the situation, humor came to Blancanales's voice. "The gang finally made their assault. They'll be searching the area for survivors. Lay low...."

"You, too," Gadgets said.

Blancanales returned the radio to his web belt. He cupped a hand around the lieutenant's ear and whispered, "We will crawl out of here, moving very, very slowly."

"But they will shoot us if we move, they will hear—"

"They will not shoot us. There is no danger. If they search for us, if they find us, I'll kill them. All the shooting—"

Slugs from a popping revolver cut through branches a few steps to their side.

"All this shooting only wastes ammunition. Now follow me. Stay close, stay low, keep your body flat and stay quiet."

A blast of birdshot tore over them, and leaves and bits of wood showered down. Blancanales moved slowly away, snaking through the darkness, never raising his body from the earth. The gang continued firing wild into the palms. From time to time Blancanales paused, waiting for Disanayake. When the young officer's hands touched his shoes, Blancanales resumed his low, slow crawl.

After a few minutes, the firing behind them stopped. Other weapons fired around the property, but none of the shots came at them. Blancanales estimated only fifty yards of brush remained between them and the road.

Flashlights moved through the palms, and Blancanales heard a machete slashing brush. The lieutenant scrambled up beside him.

"Mr. Pol! They come for us!" Disanayake said, his voice constricted with panic.

"Quiet!"

Blancanales crawled a few yards to a palm, and the lieutenant followed him. Quietly, the Politician sat against the thick cylinder of the palm's trunk and slipped out his Beretta 93-R. He thumbed back the hammer of the sound-suppressed autopistol and waited.

Three flashlights waved through the grove. Blancanales pulled down the left-hand grip lever of the Beretta and took a two-handed hold on the weapon. One flashlight came directly at them.

Light flashed from a long blade as the sword cut brush. Blancanales waited. Sword in one hand, flashlight in the other, a thug hacked a path through the undergrowth.

Lining up the three tritium dots on the darkness above the flashlight, Blancanales waited, his finger touching the trigger. The thug approached. Light flashed across Blancanales's face as the assassin continued waving the beam through the brush. He was just three steps away.

A 3-round burst slapped into the thug's chest, and the man coughed. Blancanales lined up the nightsights and fired another three shots. Slaps meant three scores. One subsonic slug continued into the distance, zipping through leaves.

The thug fell and thrashed. But he did not call out or moan. He went silent. The motionless flashlight smeared a yellow glow on the small plants and matted leaves.

"Go turn off the flashlight. Bring it here. And get that sword."

The lieutenant did not move. Blancanales kicked him.

"But he may be alive!"

Blancanales pulled out his knife. He found Disanayake's hand and pressed the knife's handle into his grasp. "Then kill him."

Finally the lieutenant moved. He went to the downed man, and Blancanales heard a fist striking flesh several times. Then the lieutenant retched. Only then did he turn off the flashlight. He retched again before returning to Blancanales.

"I killed him—" he began.

"Again."

The lieutenant passed back Blancanales's blood slick knife.

Other flashlights continued through the grove. Blancanales switched on the dead man's flashlight, and standing, he led the lieutenant to the road. There, they switched off the light and went flat where they had a view of the parked trucks. Blancanales keyed his hand radio.

"We're out."

Lyons answered, "Now we wait."

25

Bombings kill forty workers
No group claims responsibility

A probe has been launched into two mysterious explosions that killed more than forty plantation workers returning from Chilaw. The explosions destroyed the lorries as they motored south on Negombo Road.

Residents peered from their windows to see dead and dying men everywhere on the road. Officers rushing to the tragedy found the lorries burning.

Ambulance attendants attempted to give aid to the few victims still living, but, sadly, the wounded died of their terrible injuries. Doctors report the wounds indicate the employment of a new and hideous variety of sophisticated bomb.

This reporter observed unusual damage to the lorries of a nature that suggested terrorists with skills far beyond the ordinary bombthrower. Explosives had torn vast holes through the lorry cabs and the seats of the unfortunate drivers.

Officers from the Ministry of Security took personal charge of the scene when the true nature of the tragedy became known.

26

His hands fluttered like pale, translucent moths. White fingers touched his chin, his cheek, then caressed each other in a quick hand-over-hand motion.

Finally each white hand seized the other. Patrick Hansen stood at the plate-glass window viewing the Indian Ocean and the sunrise, his hands locked together in fear and desperation, like the image of a heroine in a thirties melodrama.

Hansen had the body of a woman, an old woman. White skin—a dead white, the white of the underbelly of a certain species of frog, the white of the English species—hung on pencil arms and legs. As he wrung his hands, his few muscles appeared under his dead skin, the appearance of the little strength a direct gauge of his raging nervous crisis.

The attack of the murderers had failed. Failed again. After he and Under Secretary Selvakumar had seen the Americans, identified one face-to-face! Remembering the fear of that moment made the Englishman tremble. The gang had found no one. No one! Not the one he had seen, the one who went by the strange name of the Politician, nor any of the others. They had not even found the Sri Lankan informer, Lieutenant Disanayake.

But the Americans had been there! Of course there could be no doubt. He had seen one of them, seen the shadow of another. And the destruction of the lorries proved the Americans had been nearby. Undoubtedly.

So close. Hansen trembled with the realization that the Americans had watched him. They had seen him! They must have! How could they watch the gang, avoid the searching assassins, and then place bombs on the trucks, if they had not watched the entire operation?

His trembling became shudders. They could have placed a bomb on the ministry auto. The thought of dismemberment and death made his body quake. If he had died in the flaming hulk of the Mercedes, he would not have known the pleasures of his little friend throughout the last hours of the night. Though the phone call shattered his idyll, the memory of love remained. And if he had died in the Mercedes, he would not have any chance of another attempt on the Americans.

Nor would the opportunity to take his million-dollar commission remain. The ship docked this morning. Yesterday, his contacts in the National Maritime Office reported the ship only a few miles off the coast.

The realization that he still had a chance to wrest success from defeat calmed the quivering Englishman. The Americans would try to recapture the multimillion-dollar argon ion laser and the mainframe computer. But Hansen still had a chance to make the transshipment.

If he rushed the transfer of the cargo containers....

If he assembled all the surviving thugs....

If he kept his two surviving Koreans close to his side....

If he completed every detail and fled today! Then he would be safe from the Americans who had pursued the stolen technology to this far side of the earth.

Safe to enjoy his Soviet gold.

To live like a royal prince.

27

Reading the newspaper under a wind-swaying palm, Gadgets laughed. Brilliant midday sunlight illuminated the beach, creating a tourist postcard scene of tropical beauty: deep blue waves, white beach, swaying palms and emerald-green jungle. In the distance, black monsoon clouds walled the horizon, meaning another storm in a few hours. So Gadgets enjoyed what time the monsoon allowed to sunbathe.

Strips of adhesive tape crisscrossed his arms and back, protecting the healing wounds of the Pettah gang fight from the sand and insects. Everywhere else, coconut oil shone on the healthy tan of his muscled body.

A tape of Muddy Waters wailed from his cassette player, the two voices of the bluesmaster—his guitar and his words—alien to the postcard panorama. But Gadgets grooved. He gulped from a bottle of Elephant House Stout and reread the island newspaper article describing the bombing of the trucks for the tenth time. And for the tenth time, he laughed.

His hand radio buzzed, and Gadgets reached for the radio where it lay under his shirt and pants. "Yeah?"

"The signal!" Blancanales told him. "It's the ship."

"Supercool. We work tonight. I'll come in and monitor it."

Gadgets returned to his beer and newspaper. He read through the other news. He finished the beer and popped open another. The lukewarm brown beer foamed over his hands. Then he turned over on his back to sun his face and stomach. The Muddy Waters tape ended. He hit the Eject button and put in a tape of reggae Super Smash Hits.

Shading his eyes with the newspaper, he watched the palm fronds sway, the gulls soar, the approaching wall of clouds. Then he felt the approaching footsteps.

Without moving, the electronics specialist considered the problem. One of his partners? No, Blancanales had his job in the beach house, Lyons his job standing sentry at the road. A local child? No, they either giggled and ran when they saw foreigners or came chattering and giggling to question in their strange and musical language.

Or an assassin still hanging around from last night? Maybe.

How should he kill the assassin? With the beer bottle or the newspaper? Newspaper. Why waste any more beer on the *goombas*?

As the steps neared, Gadgets moved in a blur, rolling sideways into a flying crouch, jumping, attacking Lyons with an animal scream, bringing the lethal rolled newspaper to within finger's width of the ex-cop's skull.

Lyons stared at his partner. "What's with you?"

"Don't sneak up on me. I could have killed you."

"Not with a newspaper."

"I thought you were a Sinhalese assassin. If I'd known it was you, I'd've used the overwhelming force of that beer bottle."

"You're drinking that shit?"

"I tell myself it's brewed out of peanuts. A rare exotic beer. Too strange to miss. Besides the good stuff got wasted against some *goomba*'s head."

"Why you drinking that crap when we got the signal coming in?"

The tape jammed in the cassette player. Gadgets popped open the player and examined the tape. One side had a hole the shape of the tip of an AK bayonet. Another casualty of the fight in the Pettah. Gadgets analyzed the damage and how to repair the cassette.

"What are you doing?" Lyons demanded. "The ship's here! Quit the tourist routine and pack up."

"Be cool, will you? Calm down. Let me explain what that signal means." Gadgets shook the cassette as he talked. Sometimes he paused to listen to a rattling piece of plastic inside. "The signal means the ship's in range. Maybe it's docked. Maybe it isn't. If they unload the container, we'll get a different signal. If they open the box, we'll get an alarm. So just be cool. We got all day to make it to the harbor. You want to try a midday break-in? Cruise in with our little boat, three fearless commandos and a Sinhalese lieutenant?"

Carefully shaking the cassette at a precise angle, Gadgets worked out a bit of plastic. Then he tried the tape again. It played.

"See?" Gadgets pointed at the cassette player. "Be patient and you will succeed!"

"If they open the crate, what kind of alarm do we get?"

"A different signal. Why?"

"No audio? We won't hear their voices?"

"Nah, wish we could, but we won't. Customs ain't that technologically hip. They could've set that up, but instead they risked putting a man on the ship. And they lost him."

"I want that Englishman. If we heard his voice, we'd have him."

"Why you asking about signals? Audio, video—forget the technology! By tonight we'll have established direct eyeball observation. And we've got destruction instructions; it's not like we've got to hold our fire. If that English shit shows at the box, he goes home in a box."

28

A crane took one cargo container at a time from the freighter. Patrick Hansen watched as the dock workers on the top of the next container to be unloaded took a tea break. They squatted in a circle and shared tea from a thermos, chattering and gesturing.

Hansen had watched the workers all through the day. They took tea breaks or cigarette breaks or rest breaks between every swing of the crane. They did not prepare the next container for the crane. They waited until the crane arm returned. Then the crane stood idle and the operator waited as the workers circled cables around the next cargo container and fastened the webwork of cables to the crane hook.

As a lark, he had once bought a Sinhalese-English dictionary and attempted to find several words. Efficient. Expedite. Express.

The dictionary did not list the words. At the time, Hansen had laughed and shared the joke with his English friends. But now he did not laugh.

The sun neared the horizon. The harbor workers would quit soon. And two more containers remained to be unloaded before his container could be taken from the ship. Which meant one more day before he could transfer the American equipment to a container bound for the Soviet Union.

One more day in Sri Lanka.

One more day at risk.

One more day of fear.

It was time for a bribe.

In Russian, Hansen instructed one of his Koreans to remain at the window overlooking the docks and watch for any white men approaching the freighter. Then Hansen and the other Korean left the office.

The Koreans never left his side now. His fear had not allowed him a moment of defenseless isolation at any time during the day. He had thought of stationing the Koreans on each side of his bed at night, but that would deny him the pleasures of his little lover.

Hansen went to the office of the harbormaster. Rushing past the receptionists and assistants, he threw open the door.

The harbormaster slept, his head down on his folded arms. He did not wake until Hansen closed the door, when he rose indignant.

"I say! Who exactly do you think you are? You may not simply—"

"I may and I did. This afternoon will be of great profit to you if you simply listen and follow my instructions."

The word "profit" immediately altered the man's attitude. "Sit down, my dear sir. What do you wish to discuss?"

Leaning over the desk to emphasize his quiet words, Hansen whispered, "I wish to discuss nothing. I want one favor. One and only one. Which may be difficult but which I know you can accomplish."

"But—"

"But nothing. There is a freighter down there," he said, pointing out the window that overlooked the docks. "I must have a container transferred from the freighter to the warehouse today, without delay, without excuse, without tea break. If you will do this, this is yours—"

Hansen snapped the paper of a U.S. one-hundred dollar bill. The harbormaster beamed, his round brown face like a full moon wearing glasses and a white collar.

"My dear sir! It shall be done."

The Englishman left the office before he leaped for joy.

It would all be over tonight!

29

Monsoon rain beat the plastic in a relentless roaring downpour. Wind lashed at the boat and sent storm chop smashing against the gunwales. Tied to the railings of their stolen launch, Able Team watched as the harbor lighthouse came closer every second.

They had received the second signal tone only minutes before dark, indicating the container of stolen technology had been removed from the freighter. Though the last preparations of their gear and the weatherproofing of the open launch had taken an hour, and the short sea trip from Lansiyawatta another hour in the storm, their monitor had not yet received the final signal, indicating the opening of the cargo container.

Now they looked up at the beam of the lighthouse. Only thirty yards to their right, waves crashed against the rocks of the harbor's northeast breakwater. The launch rose and fell with the swells as the lieutenant guided the small craft toward the flashing beacon lights marking the entrance to the harbor.

Squinting against the wind-driven downpour, the three Americans watched the breakwater and the lighthouse. They saw no one out in the storm.

Finally they passed the beacon. Disanayake wheeled the launch hard to the left. As the flashing beacon slid past, the swells diminished. Soon, the storm's waves died down to wind-chopped waves.

Blancanales surveyed the passing docks and cranes, then checked his plastic-laminated map of the harbor facilities. "That's the Prince Vitaya Quay, North Pier...."

Falling rain smeared the lights of the moored cargo ships. The towers and superstructures appeared as black masses against the gray night, only the indistinct blurs of lights defining the shapes.

The lights of another small craft appeared, and Disanayake cranked the wheel to the left. He killed the throttle and let the launch slide forward through the slight chop. Able Team had painted the craft black, then tented the open deck with heavy black plastic sheeting. Only the glass of the windshield remained to betray the craft.

Continuing by momentum through the water, the launch neared the vast steel wall of a freighter, the hull's steel rising from the water to loom high above them. Disanayake guided the craft slightly to the right, to a course parallel with the freighter.

The harbor-patrol boat sped past. Looking from under the plastic, Lyons saw a uniformed Sinhalese framed by a lighted window. He laughed quietly to himself, then told Gadgets, "Wait until the Tamils get smart. They'll cruise a gasoline tanker in here and shut down the harbor, in one big burn."

"Could be done...."

Disanayake restarted the engine. He weaved between the hulls of ships and the steel pilings of piers.

"There's the container terminal," Blancanales said, pointing to a line of ships. Jagged forms towered above the docks, flashing red lights warning away low-flying aircraft.

"Which one is the ship we're looking for?" Lyons asked.

"None of them," Gadgets answered. He took a receiver from his backpack. "We're looking for a warehouse, and the container in the warehouse." He flipped a switch, then a beeping tone came from the directional-impulse receiver. "Let's park this and find that laser."

Lyons turned his back to Disanayake. He whispered to Gadgets and Blancanales, "I do not like leaving him with the boat. He could—"

Blancanales shook his head. "We proved the lieutenant to be trustworthy."

"We promised him money and a visa. Maybe the English shit will pay more."

"Ironman, I've got him wired..." Gadgets countered. "There's a minimike in the boat and one taped to the inside of his raincoat. If he talks to anyone, we'll know."

"Okay," Lyons said, nodding. "Now I trust him."

"My friends!" the lieutenant called out. "I see the ladder that runs up the side of the wharf."

"Pack up!" Blancanales said to his partners.

They had come prepared. Each man of Able

Team carried a silenced pistol and an assault weapon. Lyons carried two pistols. Web gear heavy with ammunition and grenades crisscrossed their blacksuits. Though Gadgets used a lightweight Colt Automatic Rifle, he had the additional burden of electronics and explosives.

With the skill of a tour-guide helmsman, Disanayake reversed the launch and brought it backward to the ladder. "When you are gone, I will continue back under the pier, where no one will spy the craft."

"Good thinking," Blancanales told him. "And throw a sheet of plastic over the windshield. That'll totally black out the boat."

"Yes, it will be done. I hope you accomplish your investigation without violence."

"I hope so, too," Blancanales agreed.

Lyons countered with a sardonic comment. "Hopes don't count for shit. So—" He glanced at Gadgets. "What is the Boy Scout motto?"

And the two veterans of the transnational terrorist wars joined their voices in a cynical duet. "Be prepared!"

Blancanales went up first, his neoprene soles silent on the rusted steel rungs. At the last rung, he stopped and listened. He heard only the rain beating on his back. He continued to the edge of the dock.

Easing his head up, he saw a wide asphalt surface. Lights cast a gray glow on the area. Other lights illuminated the cargo doors of the warehouses beyond. Trucks and skiploaders had been parked under an awning. But two warehouses away, near an open cargo door, several vehicles lined one wall. Blancanales counted three troop transports and two Mercedes.

Snaking from the ladder, Blancanales went flat on the gray, rain-flooded asphalt, trusting the shifting shadows, the darkness, and the black of his nightsuit and weapons to conceal him. He clicked his hand radio to signal his partners.

As he waited, he watched the distant warehouse. He spotted the sentries near the trucks. Men sat in the cabs. Others stood at the tailgates. Two others patrolled the line of vehicles. He watched the roofline of the warehouse, letting his eyes glide back and forth along the gray-on-gray forms.

He spotted a sentry, an indistinct smear of black on gray that moved. Then another sentry stood next to the first. A lighter flared. The forms divided and continued on their rounds.

First Gadgets, then Lyons joined him. As Blancanales pointed out the sentries, Gadgets confirmed the warehouse as their target. Aiming the DF receiver at the warehouse, he got a full-strength signal.

"It's in there."

"With about fifty Sinhalese knifemen," Lyons added.

"They had shotguns and pistols last night," Blancanales corrected.

"Figure of speech, Pol. What's your idea on getting in there?"

"That way a hundred, two hundred yards."

Blancanales pointed in the opposite direction on the docks. "Then we cross over and work our way back. The map indicates a truck access road on the other side of the warehouse."

Gadgets nodded. "Let's go."

They crawled away. When they gained the shadows of a line of stacked containers, they walked quickly and silently along the edge of the long wharf. Once, they heard voices above them. Crewmen talked on a ship. But the three Americans went flat and snaked beneath the two men on the freighter's deck. Once past them, Able Team moved quickly again.

They paused at the end of the wharf. Pouring rain made the distant warehouse only a shadow against the darkness. They nodded to one another; no sentry there would spot them.

Dashing across the open asphalt, they continued around the corner of the last warehouse to the truck lane. There they saw a long corridor crowded with parked trucks and stacks of crated cargo. A high wall, topped with barbed wire, separated the harbor complex from Colombo. Lights along the wall illuminated the length of the truck lane.

Headlights rounded the corner from the wharf, and Able Team disappeared into the shadows and watched a patrol car pass. Two guards were inside. Able Team watched the taillights recede into the rain as the guards continued their loop.

They moved again, covering the distance in leapfrog dashes, one man watching while the other two rushed ahead. Then the first man paused and watched while the others continued. Trucks and cargo provided concealment.

Rushing the length of three warehouses, they slowed to a deliberate walk. Again, they advanced in staggered moves. But now two men watched while the third continued forward, slipping from shadow to shadow.

And now they held their silenced pistols.

Easing from behind a stack of crates, Lyons saw the sentries. He went flat on the asphalt and watched. They stood in a doorway, glancing out from time to time, the rain splattering on their black plastic hats and raincoats. When one man leaned out to scan the truck lane, Lyons saw that the sentry held a long-barreled shotgun.

Pressing himself into a space between two crates, Lyons keyed his hand radio. "We're there. I see two sentries with shotguns in a doorway. Move up slow."

Seconds later, Blancanales silently approached. The two men crouched in the darkness as rain poured down on the tarps covering the cargo.

"You see the ones on the roof?" Blancanales asked in a whisper.

"No. Only the two in the door."

"Anyone behind them?"

"Couldn't see anything."

Light swept the other side of the crates. They heard steps and the rustle of plastic. As the two black forms walked around the crates, the two crouching forms leaped up. The light touched darkness in motion, then two pistols fired simultaneously, the two Sinhalese dying as Lyons and Blancanales jerked the bodies down.

Weapons clattered on the asphalt. One dying Sinhalese choked on blood and shuddered. Lyons fired a second .45-caliber hollowpoint into the thug's head. The head jerked to the side and the body did not move again. Lyons held his hand and auto-Colt up to the rain to wash off the warm blood.

They waited, listening. They heard no footsteps or voices. Lyons turned to Blancanales.

"Raincoats and hats. Maybe we can walk through that door."

Blancanales nodded.

30

As the cardboard fell aside, Patrick Hansen saw gold. He saw the life of a randy prince of the realm. He saw an endless line of beautiful boys.

The computer stood in the litter of cardboard, the rectangles of packing foam secured with plastic tapes. No one had tampered with the multimillion-dollar mainframe.

United States customs officers had the habit of playing a nasty joke. When they intercepted a shipment, they replaced the technology with an equal weight of sandbags.

The Englishman did not want sand. So now he took the precaution of opening the crates.

He directed his Koreans to open the other cardboard cases. They used heavy knives to break the bands securing the shipping case to the pallet base. Then they carefully cut all the other tapes.

His heart beat with frantic thrusts. White hands wringing, Hansen watched the cardboard fall away.

Gleaming steel and institutional enamel appeared. Panels of foam protected the delicate components of the microlaser.

Hansen had succeeded. Tonight, the repackaged

equipment would be loaded into a cargo container bound for the Soviet Union.

Then came his gold.

At that moment, high in the steel framing of the warehouse, Gadgets Schwarz focused a camera's zoom lens on the exposed equipment. He snapped off several photos, checking the focus, zooming out to frame the entire group in the photos: the Englishman, the Koreans, the crowd of Sinhalese. Then he passed the camera to Lyons.

"Hold on to it. Keep it ready. I got to take pictures after we do this."

Lyons slipped the strap over his head. He returned his hands to the grip of his Konzak. Beside him on the platform in the framing, a magazine of one-ounce tungsten-cored slugs stood ready.

Giving his satchel charge a last check, Gadgets ran across the catwalks to a rafter directly above the open crates. He set a timer. Judging the best position, he dropped the satchel.

It hit the concrete floor in between the computer and the laser unit. All heads turned to look at the bag. Then all heads looked up to see Gadgets running for cover.

The blast sent plastic, shattered equipment and flesh everywhere. An instant later, Blancanales put a 40mm white phosphorous grenade into the chaos, spraying the wrecked computer and wounded Sinhalese with white metallic fire. Lyons did not shoot.

Rushing back to Lyons, Gadgets grabbed the camera and snapped more photos. These photos showed the total destruction of the smuggled technology. The satchel charge, two pounds of C-4 studded with hundreds of steel ball bearings, had reduced the components to trash.

Another 40mm grenade went into the open cargo container, and more phosphorous fire blazed, destroying any component left in the long aluminum box.

Finally Lyons aimed his Konzak and squeezed off single shots, eliminating the Sinhalese thugs still capable of presenting a threat. Then he jammed in another 10-round box magazine of shotshells and followed his partners in retreat.

They had done their job.

In the wreckage, Patrick Hansen tried to rise. He had not been wounded. He felt untouched. He felt ready to gather his gang and counter the American terrorist assault. But when he tried to stand, he could not get to his feet.

He pushed himself off the floor. Sitting up, he suddenly felt pain. He stayed on his side and turned, checking himself for injuries.

Then he saw the component. A long, smooth shaft of steel and plastic; Hansen recognized it as the manipulator arm of the laser.

The shaft had impaled his groin, and his every movement was bringing death closer and closer.

As the intense pain racked his body and his muscles began to twitch in reflex action, the shaft moved deeper and deeper into his insides. His silent prayers that the pain would stop with death were lost beneath his vicious screams.

MORE GREAT ACTION COMING SOON

ABLE TEAM

#19 Ironman

GUATEMALAN GRAVEYARD

Able Team's Carl Lyons travels to the cloud-swept Sierra Madre, without his partners and without his weapons.

He's met by Unomundo and his army of heartless mercs who are back in action and carving a blood-stained warpath through the ravaged country. This time Unomundo is determined to make Carl Lyons his sacrificial lamb.

But the International wants Lyons alive— at least until he leads them to the rest of Able Team.

Mack Bolan's

PHOENIX FORCE

by Gar Wilson

Schooled in guerrilla warfare, equipped with all the latest lethal hardware, Phoenix Force battles the powers of darkness in an endless crusade for freedom, justice and the rights of the individual. Follow the adventures of one of the legends of the genre. Phoenix Force is the free world's foreign legion!

"Gar Wilson is excellent! Raw action attacks the reader on every page."

—*Don Pendleton*

Phoenix Force titles are available wherever paperbacks are sold.

GOLD
EAGLE

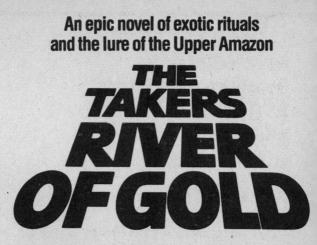

GET THE NEW WAR BOOK AND MACK BOLAN BUMPER STICKER FREE.

Mail this coupon today!